MOUNTAIN MASSACRE

ROCKY MOUNTAIN SAINT BOOK 4

B.N. RUNDELL

WOLFPACK
PUBLISHING
— EST 2013 —

Mountain Massacre
(Rocky Mountain Saint Book 4)
B.N. Rundell

Paperback Edition
© Copyright 2018 B.N. Rundell

Wolfpack Publishing
6032 Wheat Penny Avenue
Las Vegas, NV 89122

ISBN: 978-1-64119-339-9

MOUNTAIN MASSACRE

CHAPTER ONE
GRIEF

THE DIRT SPLASHED ON THE BLANKETED FORM IN THE GRAVE. Each shovelful grew heavier and the tears made it difficult to see but he struggled on with the task before him. The pile of dirt and rocks were mixed with snow and he sought to keep the snow from the form below. She had loved the snow, enjoyed watching the big flakes tumble from the pine branches and pile up around the cabin. She even enjoyed the times they used their snowshoes to trek into the lower meadows on the hunts that had become necessary this past winter. With every step of dragging those long rawhide woven snowshoes she would giggle at her clumsiness. She would stand on their porch and watch the snow sparkle under the bright sun on the frozen over lake. He remembered she seemed to take joy in almost everything they saw and everything they did together. Although they had been together for over two years, it seemed like just days. And with every shovel of dirt and frozen clumps of sod and snow, tears fell, and he felt he was burying a piece of his heart with each swing of the spade. He knew he would always see things through her eyes and feel things with her heart, for when two become one, that is what transpire in two people that are truly united, and united they were, in every facet of their lives together.

He couldn't help but remember when he first saw her, as a captive of two renegade mountain men, and the way she looked at him with hopeless and frightened eyes. He freed her and sent her back to her people, but they were destined to be together and before that year was out, they had been joined together in a ceremony among her Arapaho people and began their life together. There were so many memories, joy, happiness, fulfillment, working and playing together as they sought to build a home and prepare for a family. And now all those dreams, all those hopes, all those plans were melting with the snow under the wilting warm spring sun.

He paused and stood erect, stretched his tired back with an arch and a twist, and looked around. The grave was up the hill and behind the cabin, in a clearing where they had built a bench and would often sit and enjoy the view of the valley below. He would come to this bench for his morning time with his God and as they grew closer, they often spent that prayer time together. He leaned on the shovel, looking at the valley below, aching to be able to tell White Fawn of the herd of elk that was tip toeing from the trees and digging for the grass below. Her favorite sound in the wilderness was the bugling of the elk when they gathered their harems in the fall. He looked down, shaking his head, and returned to the task of filling in the grave.

Three weeks ago, everything was fine. She insisted on going out to check a line of snares she set for rabbits and used those clumsy snowshoes. When she crossed the small creek that led down to the lake, she struggled up the opposite bank and slid back into the creek bottom, fell and broke through the ice. It had taken her some while to free herself from the snowshoes and make it back to the cabin where

Tate was busy pouring hot lead and molding balls for his Hawken. She fell against the door, and when Tate brought her in, she was covered with ice and snow. It took the rest of the day to get her warmed up, but that was just the beginning. After almost two weeks of tending to her with all the remedies possible; chokecherry inner bark and berries in a hot tea, coltsfoot tea, and chest packs of coltsfoot and ground ivy. All proven remedies of the mountains and her congestion worsened until she could hardly talk or breathe. Every moment of suffering took the life from her eyes and the whisper from her lips as she slowly faded away until she died in Tate's arms.

He carried rocks until his hands and fingers were numb and his back ached, but he continued until the grave mound was covered. He formed a pile at the head of the grave where he would put a cross with her name, sat back on his haunches, and let the tears slide down his cheeks, turning to ice crystals in the cold air of the mountains. He dropped his head and sobbed, weeping for his White Fawn, knowing he would be empty and lost without her but also knowing she would want him to do as she told him with almost her last breath, *Live, you must live, for both of us, live here in our mountains. Have a life, maybe another woman, but know I am always with you.*

He slowly stood, hands loosely holding the shovel, wiped his face, sniffled, and sucked in a deep breath and walked toward the cabin. His big wolf, Lobo, trailed along beside him, head hanging low, as if he also missed the woman that played with him and loved on him. He would finish the cross, now sitting beside the table in the cabin. When he placed the marker at her grave, he would read the scriptures and say goodbye to his beloved White Fawn. He stumbled down the incline, stood the shovel by the lean-to shelter of the horses, walked to the cabin and entered the welcome warmth. But it was empty. He stood just inside the door and looked at the dusty shafts of sunlight bending into the window, and everything was the same, but it was empty. She had filled this cabin with her smiles, her laughter, her presence, but now it was empty. His shoulders slumped, and he fell into the chair, reaching for the crude form of the cross and started carving.

"*Let not your heart be troubled; ye believe in God, believe also in me. In my Father's house are many mansions: if it were not so I would have told you. I go to prepare a place for you. And if I go and prepare a place for you, I will come again, and receive you unto myself; that where I am, there ye may be also.*" Tate read the words aloud as he stood at the grave and looked down at the rocks, longing to see the smiling face of White Fawn, trying to picture her before him. He began to pray, "Lord, I'm hurting now, and I don't understand, but I'm doin' my best to trust, but you're gonna hafta help me." He continued praying and pouring out his heart and his grief, choked back more sobs as he straightened up and lifted his eyes to the tree tops and the blue sky beyond, forcing a smile as he remembered White Fawn lifting her hands to the sky and expressing her happiness at every new day. He thought to himself how he was going to have to work at understanding that kind of joy but for now, he wasn't feeling so happy.

They had planned on making a trip for supplies come spring and he knew he would have to do that, he was running low on many things and out of some things. He liked living in the mountains, but he hadn't found the makings for black-powder, sugar, and flour. He knew there were deposits of galena, although he hadn't found any yet, and there were many plants and herbs about, but he hadn't mastered the making of flour. He had used honey in place of sugar, but it wasn't quite the same. He knew there were other things that were needed, but he would have to take some time to make a list, something that had been White Fawn's responsibility. The trails would be open soon, at least the one back to South Pass, and he needed to be ready before the mud got too deep to travel, like usually happened in mid-spring or later. He rubbed Lobo behind his ears, stroked the thick fur at his neck, and said, "We're all alone now, boy. Just us." He turned his attention to his gear and began taking inventory of his needs, time would soon be upon him and he had to be ready.

Spring in the mountains is a combination of cold nights and sun filled days. While the welcome warmth does its best to melt the snow, the drifts often recede to the shadows and hold on well into the warmer months. Frozen ground, once revealed after snow's retreat, quickly diminish into soggy bottomed trails as the spring flowers race one another for the first rays of spring sun. Trees that stood brittle in cold temperatures that held even the air hostage now course with warm sap and branches begin waving in the mild breezes. The bare-boned aspen anxiously push forth new pale green sprouts to contrast with the white bark of the scarred trunks that bear the stories of elk and deer rubbing the velvet from their antlers in the previous late summer. Tate rode Shady, his dark grey grulla with black legs, mane and tail, and led Speckles, the appaloosa that was White Fawn's favorite and the long legged black gelding. Both were rigged with pack-saddles, panniers and parfleche. Although most of the packs were empty in anticipation of the re-supply, the appaloosa carried enough gear and supplies for this trip.

Tate was outfitted with his usual armament; the Hawken

in the scabbard under his right leg, his longbow and quiver in a sheath under his left leg, his Bowie in a sheath at the small of his back, his metal bladed tomahawk in his belt at his right hip, and the Paterson Colt in its holster, butt forward on his left hip. These are the weapons that had served him well and his proficiency with them all had been repeatedly proven. It had never been his purpose to become known, desiring only to be a solitary figure, unobserved and unknown. But the name Tate Saint had become synonymous with Rocky Mountain Saint, after many occasions of helping those that were in trouble or difficulty. Perhaps the best known being his rescue of a group of missionaries that had been waylaid by renegade trappers that Tate had hunted down and exacted retribution. But when he took White Fawn as his wife, they both wanted to spend their lives away from everyone and raise a family in the ways of the mountains. Now Tate was bound for Fort William and maybe a reunion with his old friends, Sublette and Fitzpatrick, and he was hopeful of seeing Carson again as well. Kit had become a mentor to Tate when he first came to the mountains, and the two had met up again at a rendezvous when he and Kit had taken wives of the Arapaho. The women had been close friends and the time together was memorable.

When he broke from the trees on the flat at the crest of the trail that had become known as South Pass, he moved farther into the open and reined up to take in the view of the wide-open plains beyond. As far as he could see, there was the rolling terrain, spotted with clusters of juniper and piñion, flat topped and rim-rocked mesas, different mountain ranges in the distance, all arched over by a crystalline blue sky devoid of any clouds. The sun stood off his left shoulder and seemed to be working overtime to turn the snowbanks into rivulets and streams that would wash the gullies and arroyos clear of winter's accumulation. He noticed a patch of little blue-bell looking flowers, mostly buds, but all reaching for the sun. Beyond that patch was another with taller stems and yellow pea type flowers already showing an abundance of blossoms. These were the sights that always made White Fawn stop and usually get down to take a blossom to her nose to enjoy the fresh fragrance of the mountains. He lifted his shoulders as he breathed deeply, raised his eyes to the trail before him and gigged his mount forward. Lobo was patiently staying at his side, often looking up at the man, searching for any signal or command and seeing none, scanned the terrain for any mischief he could tackle.

As they traveled, Tate would take the less exposed trail, keeping himself as inconspicuous as possible. Although he was not concerned for his safety, confident in his abilities and those of his animals, it was always best not to push your luck. There were always dangers, most unseen, whenever traveling in the wilderness alone. Dangers came in the form of men, animals, and the country itself. And it always ha a way of coming upon you unannounced and with little fanfare. And the mountains are not gentle in their teaching, nor are the lessons easily learned.

Carson had told Tate of the route to Sublette's Fort William when they were together, and Tate had to reach back in his memory to draw out the map imprinted there about two years prior. "Just foller that Sweetwater east a couple days or so, an' when it turns north, just keep ona goin' due east. That'll take ya' o'er a row o' purty good foothills, an' ya' should come out on th' Laramie river, it might be a touch to th' south. An' ya' can foller it right into th' fort! From up hyar," and he was on the crest of South Pass when he gave the instructions, "it'll take ya' mebbe a couple weeks, give or take." Carson often lapsed into the vernacular of the mountains, although he was known to be a knowledgeable though illiterate man. Carson pointed to a draw below them and said, "That thar's Slaughterhouse gulch, an' if'n ya foller it on down, it'll take ya' ta' the Sweetwater. But if'n I was you, I'd just head off down yonder an' you'll pick up the Sweetwater out thar where it flattens out a little. Easier goin' thataway." Tate pointed the grulla to the flats and by midday, had a good start on his journey.

The two weeks were made more pleasant by the rapid coming of spring. Graze for the animals was plentiful, game along the river was easily taken, and the weather held nothing but blue sky and warm days. The abundance of color, whether patches of flowers along the riverside or clusters of prickly pear cactus with big yellow blossoms and cholla with deep pink flowers, kept the memory of White Fawn ever before him. She would never miss an opportunity to point out new buds and blossoms and took pleasure in every new color displayed.

He sat, leaning on the pommel of his saddle, looking at the fort below. The horses were snatching mouthfuls of grass and Lobo had dropped to his belly as they waited for Tate to drink his fill of the sight of the trading fort called Fort William. Named after William Sublette, the fort had tall walls of vertical timbers, ported bastions on opposing corners, and an overhanging bastion that rested on two big timbers and shaded the main entry gate. Two groups of tipis were gathered downstream and on the flat beyond the fort, separated by a good distance which told they were of different tribes. Two different herds of horses were watched over by several mounted figures assumed to be boys of the tribes. There was no shortage of people and activity in and about the fort.

Tate came off the hilltop, crossed the river and pointed his horses to the entryway of the fort. Any new figure was watched by those nearby, most disinterested but curious, and the sight of a wolf tagging along beside this man was an unusual sight indeed. Tate kept his eyes on the gate, doing his best to ignore those he passed. Once inside, he easily spotted the hub of activity, the traders store, and reined up at an empty hitch rail. The past few years with the work of clearing timber, hauling and hoisting logs to build cabins and corrals, handling animal carcasses, and the usual work of the mountains, had given Tate a well-developed torso. Broad shoulders strained at the buckskin shirt and light brown hair covered his collar. He stood a couple inches over six feet and carried a good 175 pounds of muscle. Preferring to be clean shaven, his face showed his youth, but his eyes showed his wisdom and experience. His walk told of his confidence and his weapons told of his danger. He wrapped the reins over the hitch rail and stepped up on the boardwalk to enter the trader's store. He paused at the open doorway, letting his eyes adjust to the darker interior as he breathed in the smells of the store; the combination of trade goods, hides and pelts, and unwashed bodies. It was an unpleasant stench but one that had to be endured. Three tables to the left, partially obscured in the shadows and smoke, caught the dusty sun rays that fought their way through the fly specked window. Two tables held three men each and the third had two men, all watching the goings on of the trader and others. Tate stepped to the far side away from the tables, looking at the goods stacked along the wall.

Hanging on the wall were several traps of assorted size and make and several coils of braided rope. Tate started to reach for one of the ropes and a very loud and gruff voice from slightly behind him hollered, "Hey, gitchur hands away from tha' trap! Thash my trap!"

Tate turned to look at the source of the noise, saw a man in dirty buckskins, full beard, and a thick head of hair that seemed to go in all directions at once. He was a burly brute, easily as tall as Tate but wider in the beam, and he reeked of whiskey. He weaved back and forth and snarled again at Tate, "Gitchu younker! Thish place iss for men!" he declared holding up a fist before his face, threatening Tate. Tate turned to face the man just as the drunk started a round house swing at his head. Without a word, Tate ducked under the swing, caught the sleeve of the swinging arm and twisted it around behind the man, spinning him on his toes. With the man's arm behind his back, Tate walked him to the open doorway and pushed him through, watching him stumble off the boardwalk, bounce off a hitchrail and fall face first in the dust. Tate grinned as the man tried unsuccessfully to get to his feet, then Tate turned and stepped back into the room, where several silent and surprised men looked at the young man as if he had done some terrible deed. Tate paid little attention to the others and waited for the trader to finish with the men before him.

He felt a tap on his shoulder and after a quick glance from the corner of his eye, he turned to see one of the men that had been seated, standing behind him. "Say young fella, could we buy you a drink?" as he motioned to the other men at the table. All were looking expectantly at Tate and he looked back at the man and said, "No, thanks, but I don't drink."

The man appeared surprised and asked, "Whatsamatta, you got some kinda religion or sumpin'?"

"It's not that. I tried it, didn't like it, so I don't drink it. Simple as that."

"Oh, well, then how 'bout some coffee? Ya drink coffee, don'tcha?"

Tate grinned at the man and said, "Yes, I drink coffee. But, I need to put in my order for some supplies first, if that's alright?" He had caught the signal from the trader and stepped to the counter. As he turned his attention to the trader, he saw the man return to the table and the three men watched as he gave the trader the list of goods he wanted to purchase. Tate wondered what the men wanted, and he casually looked them over while he waited on the trader. They appeared honest enough, at least they didn't look like a bunch of renegades or cutthroats, but he wasn't sure he wanted to spend any more time among people than he absolutely had to, but, it might be good to talk a spell, catch up on things going on in the world. He decided he would at least listen to see if they had something special in mind. He didn't have to give them any more than a little time, after all.

WHILE HE SETTLED UP WITH THE TRADER, TATE NOTICED THE men at the table had their heads together, speaking with one another in whisper tones, and he wondered what they had to say that was such a secret. He tucked the pouch that still held a few coins under his belt and picked up an armload of goods and started toward the door. When the man that invited him to join them for a drink saw him turn to leave, he scrambled to his feet and said, "Here, let us help you with that. Since you don't drink anyway, we'll just give you a hand." He nodded to his table mates and they went to the counter and gathered up more of Tate's goods and followed him out the door.

Tate noticed the troublemaker was leaned up against the boardwalk and was apparently sound asleep. A sudden snort followed by a ripsaw snore affirmed his judgment and Tate moved to his pack horses. He began packing the panniers on the black and continued as the other men sat their parcels on the pile to await packing. While Tate busied himself, the men gathered around and the spokesman for the group began, "The reason we wanted to talk to you, uh, oh, by the way, my name is Henry Hyde, and this is Ed Bowman and Chuck Heaton. We're with the wagons out yonder." Tate nodded his head to each of the men as their names were given and continued his packing. "Well, that man you bull rushed out the door, he's called Bear, an' he was our guide or wagonmaster." Tate looked at the men over his shoulder and waited for more. "We wanted to thank you." Tate dropped his hands to his side and turned to the men and with his brow wrinkled in question replied, "Thank me?"

"Yes, you see, he has been bullying everyone ever since we were about a week out of St. Joe, that's where we're from, St. Joe, Missouri. Anyway, he's been bullyin' everyone, but we couldn't get rid of him cuz we didn't have anyone else to guide us." He left the thought hanging as if expecting a response from Tate, but with none forthcoming, he continued, "And when we seen whatchu done, we thought you might be just the man to take us on through."

Tate turned to look at the men again, letting his eyes go from one to the other, and asked, "Through to where?"

"Why, to Oregon territory, of course. We're hopin' to stake us out some farms in that country. What we hear is there's lots o' good land that'd make right fine farms. That's what we're wantin', cuz we're all farmers."

"No kiddin'?" asked Tate, as if he couldn't tell they were farmers from their get-ups.

The men looked at one another and at Tate, and he asked, "And what makes you think . ." Suddenly a shout from the boardwalk got their attention, "Tate! Tate! Why you rascal, you. I thought you'd never leave them mountains!" Tate looked to see Sublette hopping from the boardwalk, using a gnarly walking stick as an aid, and with an outstretched hand and a broad smile splitting his face. Tate was excited to see the man and stepped toward him, "Bill, you ol' houn' dog!" and the two men came together in a mountain man bear hug, slapping each other on th back and laughing. Sublette pushed the young man back, held him at arms-length and looking around asked, "Well I see you still got that mangy wolf, but where's White Fawn?"

Tate dropped his head and said, "Gone under, Bill, less'n a month back. Dunno if it was the Gripp or the fever, but she just wasted away, nuthin' I did helped." He shook his head at the memory and looked up at Sublette to see sympathetic eyes and felt his hand on his shoulder.

Sublette looked at the men nearby and back at Tate and asked, "So, whatchu gonna be doin' now? You ain't leavin' the mountains are ya?"

Tate looked at his friend with surprise showing and said, "Of course not! I'm just down here gettin' supplies's all."

"Oh," and he looked at the other men and started to turn away but one of the men asked, "Mr. Sublette, would you recommend this man as a guide to get us to Oregon?"

"Well, off hand, I don't know of anyone that knows that country better'n Tate here." He looked at his friend and asked, "So, thinkin' of guidin' some pilgrims are ye?"

"I ain't doin' no such thing! I din't even know that's what they wanted!" he declared as he looked from Sublette to the others. He shook his head and resumed his packing, mumbling to himself.

Sublette chuckled and said, "Well, come see me 'fore ya leave, now, y'hear?"

"Yeah, sure. I allus' want to see muh friends 'fore I leave!" Tate snorted at Sublette, disgusted with his recommendation as if he had been betrayed. He watched as Sublette mounted the boardwalk and walked away to what Tate assumed were his quarters. When he turned back to his rigging of the packs, the men stepped closer and said in a low tone, "We can pay you and with Mr. Sublette's recommendation we'll pay you top wages to take us through."

Tate turned, rested his right arm on a pack as he leaned against the horse, looked at the men and said, "Look, I have never been a guide, I have no hankerin' to be a guide, and there's nothing about guiding that appeals to me at all. Now, I have all the supplies I need, and I don't need a job, so how 'bout you findin' someone else to pamper you pilgrims across this country."

"But you don't understand, is it Tate? Is that what Mr. Sublette called you, Tate?"

"Yes, my name is Tate."

"Well, Mr. Tate," and he was interrupted with, "Not Mr. Tate, just Tate." "What you don't understand is, there is no one else. We've been hoping to find someone, but all there has been is Indians and a few trappers that are going back to St. Louis. Bear and his helper, Gramps, are the only ones and we cannot abide that man any longer. He is of absolutely no help, he's always drunk, bullying someone, making unreasonable demands and is totally disrespectful of our womenfolk. They refuse to go any further with that man!"

Tate had noticed the three men that had been at the table with Bear had come from the trader's supply and had helped the man up and were walking him toward the livery, each man with a shoulder under each arm. When Tate looked back, Hyde resumed his argument, "We were also suspicious that he had plans to rob us and leave us. He had asked about our supplies and if we had money to get more and well, other things, that just made us concerned."

Tate looked at the men and thought about others he had known when he lived with his family in Missouri. His father had told him that most of the people liked civilization because they had someone else to fight their battles for them. He said they hired others as law officers, soldiers, and just about every other distasteful job would have someone willing to do another's work for pay. As Tate looked these men over, they appeared able enough, farming was hard work, and it took men and made men. But even farmers, at least those in the states, had become accustomed to law officers tending to the unruly and unlawful, so they could tend to the farm. As he looked at the men, who were but a sampling of those with the wagons, he shook his head and said, "Look, all I can do is say I'll think it over." The men immediately acted as if he had agreed and he held up his hand and said, "Don't go jumpin' to conclusions! I just said I'd think about it. That country out there is tougher and meaner'n anything you've come across so far. Ain't many wagons, mostly traders like Sublette an' others, ever made it. There's more things out there that'll bitecha, stingya, kickya, an' killya, than you've ever seen before. There's buffalo an' grizzly bears as big as your wagon and rattlesnakes as long as that wagon, scorpions bigger'n your hands, spiders big as your hat and that'll jump three feet high. Why, the jackrabbits stand as tall as your armpits and have feet big 'nuff to slap your momma! No sir, I just said I'd think it over. But you need to be thinkin' it over too!"

The men stood, mouths agape at the descriptions that flowed from this man that had seemed to be a quiet sort, and now he told of things they never imagined. When he finished, they closed their mouths, looked at one another and silently walked away. Tate watched as they left, chuckling to himself and his imitation of his old friend, Knuckles. He finished the lashing of the packs, led the horses to a water trough, found some shade for the animals and walked to the quarters of Sublette.

When Tate knocked at the door, "Enter!" barked from inside and he walked in to be greeted again by Sublette. The founder of the fort had a Crow woman tending to his quarters and he motioned for her to bring them some coffee. At Sublette's nod, Tate seated himself in front of a rectangular table, loaded with crude maps and papers. As he pushed them aside to set his coffee cup down, Sublette asked, "So, ya gonna guide them pilgrims?"

Tate shook his head and said, "Thanks for that recommendation. You coulda just said I couldn't be trusted and that'd be the end of it, an' I could go home to my mountains with a clear conscience."

Sublette chuckled, his chest rising with the laughter, and said, "Well, they seem like good folks. They been here a few days, ain't been anybody else come through, at least anybody goin' thataway," he motioned with a raised arm in the direction of the western mountains.

"What's wrong with the one they had, I mean, I know they don't like him but since when are guides supposed to be their best friend?"

Sublette turned serious and said, "Well, I don't know anything good about Bear, but I do know that for three rendezvous runnin' that one called Gramps came in with a big load o' pelts and minus any partners. But each year 'fore that he left with two or three partners, but come tradin' time, partners come up missin'," explained Sublette. "Ever time I asked, he had some story 'bout accidents, Indians, or they plum' run-off or sumpin', always had an excuse. Got to where nobody'd partner up wit' him. I was s'prised to hear him an' Bear was guidin' them pilgrims."

"Humm, now you're tryin' to make me feel sorry for 'em," drawled Tate.

"Well, I ain't tellin' ya' what to do, but, if you decide to take 'em, you be sure to watch yore back. They been hangin' 'round a couple others that I wouldn't trust neither, especially that half-breed, I think they call him Hoots. He's a renegade Sioux, got run out from them cuz he was cuttin' up their own women. Cain't trust a man like that, don't care if'n he's red or white or . . . " he held his hands up at his sides to express his disgust.

"Now, are you tryin' to talk me into goin' with them, or talkin' me outta goin'? Cuz if you're try to talk me outta goin', you purt' near got me convinced."

Tate sipped his coffee, sat the cup down and asked, "Say, did you ever hear from them missionaries?"

Sublette grinned and said, "Yup, after my man got 'em up north a ways, he handed 'em off to some Hudson Bay boys and they took 'em on to Blackfoot and Cayuse country. They got their mission goin', a school started, and last I heard, they were doing right well."

Tate grinned at the report, glad to hear the friends he helped through the Wind River mountains had reached their destination safely. The two couples were missionaries and the women were the first white women to make it through the mountains and over that portion of what would become the Oregon trail. Narcissa Whitman and Eliza Spalding and their husbands Marcus and Henry, built a thriving mission work among the Cayuse, Nez Perce, and Blackfoot Indians and cared for many of the children.

Tate had become wistful for a moment, lifted his eyes to Sublette and knew his moment had been seen as Sublette said, "Yeah, I think of 'em often too. They're good people an' you sure helped 'em out of a jam up there in them mountains. If it wasn't for you, there would be several more unmarked graves in the high lonesome."

Tate looked at Sublette and read his unspoken message in those words, knowing the man was saying he had to help these pilgrims or there would be many more unmarked graves. He shook his head, remembering the words of his Pa, "If someone needs your help and you can give it, don't dally, just get busy with the doin' of it."

Tate sucked in a deep breath that lifted his shoulders, stood to his feet and shaking his head, he extended his hand to Sublette. The two men shook hands without saying another word. Tate walked from the room, looking to his horses and went to fetch the animals and started walking them to the gate.

CHAPTER FOUR
PREPARATIONS

HE NO SOONER STEPPED THROUGH THE BIG ENTRY GATE THAN he was greeted enthusiastically by Henry Hyde. Tate was leading his grulla and the pack-horses trailed behind while Lobo walked beside Shady. Hyde had not seen the wolf before and at first sight, he stepped back putting Tate between him and the beast as he asked, "Is that with you?" pointing to the big wolf, now sitting on his haunches beside his four-legged friend. Tate glanced back at Lobo and as a grin spread across his face he looked at Hyde and asked, "You might say that. Sometimes I think the rest of us are with him. Is that a problem?"

An obviously nervous Hyde looked from Tate to the wolf and muttered, "Uh, I suppose not, he just surprised me is all. It ain't everyday I see a wolf, and especially not one that big or this close up." He looked at Tate again and asked, "So, does this mean you're accepting our offer?"

"Maybe, but first I need to take a look at your animals and equipment."

"Oh, certainly, certainly, I'm sure everything will meet with your approval. Bear made sure we were outfitted properly, at least he did that right," commented the man, obviously still disgusted with the drunkard bully.

As they approached the wagon camp, Tate visually and thoroughly took in everything. Nine wagons meant nine families, maybe a dozen guns he thought. The animals were in a bunch just past the wagons and from what he could tell at this distance, most were mules, which was expected with these people being farmers. Mules were better for farm work, plowing and such, and would be more dependable on the trail. He started walking around the wide circle, accompanied by Hyde, and gave a cursory look at the wagons and harnesses. The wagons were the standard farm wagon type with bows and bonnets, what were often called prairie schooners because of the white canvas bonnets that resembled the sails of the schooners on the high seas. All seemed to be in good repair, several carrying spare wheels and other parts, grease buckets dangling underneath, harnesses in good repair and well oiled, all what he expected from farmers that knew the need of maintaining their equipment.

Completing the circle, Tate spoke to Henry, "How 'bout gatherin' the folks together and let's talk a bit, whatsay?"

Tate leaned against a wagon, one foot on the tongue and an arm resting on the box, as he watched the families gather. Nothing unusual about any of them, all seemed to be typical farmer types, strong and hardy, what his Ma used to call "sturdy." There were several children and he noted a couple of young men, obviously older children of some of the mature couples. As they settled down, many having brought stools or chairs, Henry Hyde stood before them and began, "As most of you know, we decided to change guides. We asked Tate here," he motioned to Tate and looked at him, "by the way, what is your full name?"

"Tate Saint," replied Tate without volunteering anything additional.

"Yes, Tate Saint, we asked him to take over as guide and he has agreed to consider the job after he talks with all of us. He has already looked over the wagons, some of you met him then, and the stock and now he wants to talk with all of us together." He looked at Tate and motioned for him to step forward, and Hyde sat down on a stool next to a woman that Tate assumed was his wife.

"Well, folks, you need to understand that I didn't come lookin' for this job. Your men here," motioning to Henry and the others nearby, "came to me about it. Now, I've never been with a wagon train, but I know that country," nodding his head toward the far mountains, "and I've been around these parts a few years now. But what I want you to know is what you're gonna be up against after you leave here. That country to the west of here is far different from back yonder," waving his hand to the east, "and the critters that inhabit that country are different. You'll find it dryer, always blowin' dust, hot sun, cold nights, an' the trail ain't been used much by wagons, cepin' the trade wagons that go to the rendezvous. There'll be days you travel from dawn to dark an' it'll look like you ain't hardly moved, cuz it seems like everything's the same. It's gonna be hard goin' an' you need'ta know that 'fore you leave here. This here's the last place you can get supplies, so if you run outta sumpin' that's yore tough luck cuz there ain'tny more places to get nuthin'. If sumpin' breaks, an' you can't fix it, too bad. Some of you'll get sick, and some of you'll prob'ly die. That land out there has plenty of unmarked graves and there'll be lots more. Now, any you got questions for me?"

A big man at the back that Tate had noticed with a scowl on his face and showing restlessness, raised his hand and Tate saw the big hand was on the end of an arm that looked more like a log and with as much thick black hair as the bark on a log. He looked at the man, bald head with a thick patch of fur over his ears and a full beard that hid his neck, thick eyebrows that shadowed his black eyes and he spoke with a growl when he asked, "What 'bout Bear and Gramps?"

Tate found out later that this man was the only one that seemed to get along with Bear, probably because he was every bit as big as the man called Bear and just as intimidating. Tate looked at Henry for the answer to the man's question, and Henry stood, "Lucas, after talking it over, we," motioning to several other men, "agreed that Bear's services were no longer needed. We wanted someone that knew the country and wasn't drunk all the time."

"He ain't gonna like it!"

Suddenly from behind the wagon came a growl of a voice that shouted, "That's for sure an' certain! An' if you pilgrims think you can get rid o' me, you got another think a'comin'!" Pushing his way through the group near the back of the wagons was Bear, followed close behind by the one known as Gramps. Bear shoved people, men and women alike, aside and stepped in front of Henry Hyde and said, "Sides, you still owe me. Our deal was half up front an' the rest when we get there."

Tate had to give Henry credit for standing up to the big man when he responded, "That's just it, Bear, we're not 'there' as you put it, and you've been paid for what you've done. Now, you're through. Tate there is going to be our guide from here on out!"

Bear growled as he spun around to face Tate, arms spread wide as if he was going to grab the man that threatened to take his job. When he saw Tate, he said, "You! Ha! You ain't nuthin' but a young pup! You ain't takin' nobody nowhere! An' that's final! Now run on home to your momma, pup!" He took a step toward Tate, threatening, but was stopped when he heard a growl. He looked down to see Lobo, hackles up, fangs bared, and muzzle snarled as he growled at the big man. Bear stepped back and said, "That's a wolf! Where's muh rifle?" as he turned back to Gramps, never letting his eyes leave the threatening Lobo. His partner extended the rifle toward him and the searching hand grasped the fore stock, pulling the rifle forward as Tate slapped it aside. Bear was shocked at the sudden blow that knocked the rifle from his hands and scowled at the young man before him, now dropped into a slight crouch, waiting for Bear's next move.

The big man surprised him, moving faster than expected as he charged Tate with arms wide expecting to grab him in a bear hug and squeeze the life from him. Tate quickly ducked under the man's arm and kicked at the side of his knee, making him fall forward into the dirt. When he hit the ground, he grabbed at his knee, howling and moaning, "You broke muh leg! I'm gonna kill you for this!"

Tate knelt beside the man, out of his reach and spoke softly to the big man, "No, you're not gonna be killin' anybody. Your partner here's gonna help you up and back to your camp and you'll leave these folks be, otherwise, next time I'll have to either let Lobo have at'chu or I'll have to kill you myself." Tate stood up and motioned for Gramps to help his friend and leave. He watched as the two men, one hobbling on one foot, left the crowd and disappeared behind the wagons, making their way to their own camp.

Tate stood before the wagon and looked at the crowd and asked, "Any questions?"

The people of the wagons relaxed, and a few started asking questions, most of which were simple like what kind of animals were to be expected, what the country was like, how long until they reach the real mountains, and before long, most were ready to retire to their wagons and finish preparations in anticipation of leaving at first light. Henry stepped to his side and said, "I'm almighty grateful that you decided to join us, Tate. After what Bear said, I was afraid of what might happen, but you handled it just fine, yes sir, you sure did." Tate knew they hadn't seen the last of Bear and his bunch, but there was little they could do about it now. He would just have to heed the advice of Sublette and watch his back.

CHAPTER FIVE

TATE SAT WITH HIS FOREARMS LEANING ON THE SADDLE HORN as he watched the wagons start to pull out. The mules, responding to slapped reins, bullwhips, buggy whips, thrown pebbles and shouts from the drivers, leaned into their harness, pulling the trace chains taut and the wagons creaked in protest as they were pulled from the ruts of the past few days sitting at rest. He didn't remember all the names, but some came to mind as they passed him by, following the lead wagon driven by Henry Hyde. Most of the couples sat side by side, husband with the lines, all showing an eagerness and excitement at finally getting on the trail again. When the fifth wagon came abreast of Tate's horses, he was surprised to see a woman with the reins and seated alone on the springboard seat. Riding alongside were two men, one apparently the husband and the other a young man, probably their son. As he watched, another young man, about the same age, rode up alongside and began talking with the pair. Tate would find out later he was the son of the Hillyard's, whose wagon was two back from this one. The woman appeared quite capable of handling the four-up team of mules and she occasionally snapped a buggy whip with a loud crack, each time startling the mules and getting a slight hump in response. Tate watched until he saw the last wagon moving, noticed it was driven by the big man, Lucas, who he was told was the only one that was not a farmer, but a blacksmith.

Tate gigged his mount forward, kicked him up to a trot and with taut lead lines, the three horses soon overtook the lead wagon and passed them by, moving out to scout the trail before them. Lobo trotted alongside, tongue lolling out and looking to Tate as if he was smiling and happy they were on the move again. In a short while, he pulled the animals back to a walk, and he surveyed the countryside. Although he had traveled a more direct route, following the Laramie river from the nearby mountain range, at the advice of Sublette, he was taking the wagon train on the previously traveled route of the trade wagons and what would later become known as the Oregon Trail. This route would circumvent many of the mountains and would be easier traveling for the wagons as well as staying near the North Platte River and a continuous source of water.

Tate stayed on the scout, leaving it to Henry and the others to pick a site for their nooning and the pace they wanted to travel. He would watch how they managed the train, order of travel, night camps, and more, before he would make any recommendations. He knew he had been hired to take them across, which meant mostly that he was to point the way, but they also expected him to have their safety foremost in his mind regarding any decisions as to where and when they would travel. Tate had always been a man to consider all the possibilities and problems before he set about any task and he had learned to be cautious in all of his decisions. Life in the mountains, with all its challenges and dangers, made a man careful because anything could quickly injure or kill in the wilderness. And usually, there was no one around to help a man out of whatever predicament he found himself in, and that knowledge naturally made a man wary of just about anything.

As he rode, he catalogued all the territory in his mind, a practice of all men of the mountains, for that knowledge could one day save his life. He saw a small herd of antelope, several deer, a few hungry coyotes on the prowl, jackrabbits taking their meal on fresh green sprouts, and he bypassed a large prairie dog village. The low rolling hills held an abundance of wildlife, but most of the vegetation was cactus, bunch grass, sagebrush, and an occasional juniper, and cedar. The wide-open vistas stretched beyond the limits of his eyesight, and the distant horizon was barely discernible by shaded blue of the low sky. Overhead, the expansive cobalt sky was void of clouds and held the brilliant sun at its lowest arch having almost completed its daily journey. He noted a wide depression that straddled a shallow dry wash with low ridges and knolls around that would provide some shelter and thought this would be the site for their night camp. Several clusters of juniper marked the edge and there was ample graze of the buffalo grass and some gramma for the animals. The edge of the depression was bordered by the riverbank and its scattered willows and alder, with a sloping bank to the water providing easy access for both animals and people.

Henry had asked Tate to choose the first night's camp and if possible, take some game for fresh meat. "Since we been at the fort, we haven't had a chance to get fresh meat, and some venison steaks broiled o'er the fire'd sure taste good," said the man as he waved at the departing Tate. After giving his horses water, he stripped off their gear, hobbled them and set up his camp by the alders. He slipped his longbow from the sheath and strung the bow, hung the quiver on his pistol holster and started upstream, looking for deer coming down to the river for their evening water. It was just a short while later that he saw several deer tiptoeing from a brushy ravine, making their way to the riverside. He had stationed himself in a thicket of willows, affording himself cover and room enough to take his shots. He waited until the group of five deer, two button bucks, two does and a yearling, reached the water and warily took their drink. They were less cautious as they began to graze at the greener grass on the riverbank and Tate slowly stood to start his draw. Careful to move only when their heads were down or turned away, he stepped into the bow taking it to full draw and let the first arrow fly to silently take the first buck, embedding itself to the fletching in the lower chest, just behind the front leg. An instant kill shot, and the deer dropped without taking a step, but before the buck hit the ground, Tate had another arrow on its way to take the second buck before it could be spooked. When that spike buck staggered and fell, the three other deer launched themselves with long bouncing leaps and within seconds were gone. They disappeared into the brushy draw without the slightest sound, only that of small hooves giving footing for each springing jump. Tate waited just a moment, then started to the downed animals to begin the task of dressing the deer to return them to camp.

When he returned to his camp with one of the carcasses, he saw the wagons approaching and he dropped the deer, slipped his bow back into the sheath, put his quiver and bow with the rest of his gear and waved at the first wagon as he walked from the shade of the two cottonwoods at the edge of the stream. Henry grinned at their guide as he walked up to the wagon, and as Tate told Henry about the camp, he motioned in the direction of the suggested campsites. Henry slapped the reins to the mules and as he turned his wagon, he waved at the others to follow and in short order, the wagon train was stopped for the night. Tate told Henry about the deer at his camp and that he would retrieve the second one while they set up their camp and Henry's wife, Susan, said, "Now we expect you to join us for supper, now y'hear?" Tate grinned and waved at the woman as he nodded his head and walked away to retrieve the deer. He heard someone coming behind him and he looked around to see a boy of about twelve or thirteen, running to catch up as he asked, "Mr. Saint, can I come with you?"

"I s'pose that'd be alright. And who might'chu be?"

"I'm Hank. Henry Hyde's muh Pa," declared the boy as he stretched out to catch up with their scout and guide. "So, ya got a deer didja?" he asked.

"Got a couple of 'em, one's over yonder in my camp there, and the other'ns upstream a short way."

The boy looked at Tate, noticed he wasn't carrying a rifle and asked, "Well, how'dja get 'em, you ain't carryin' no rifle?"

"Well, these mule deer out here in the wilds, they're mighty spooky, an' if'n ya' sneak up on 'em just right, you can jump outta the brush and scare 'em and they'll just fall over dead."

The boy turned his head to the side and looked at Tate to see if he was serious, and with Tate showing no expression at all, he finally said, "You're joshin' me ain'tchu?"

Tate chuckled and rubbed the top of the boy's head and said, "Yup, sure am. But it made'ja think, though, didn't it?"

Hank laughed and said, "Yeah, but I knew you couldn't be serious 'bout it. Ain't no deer gonna fall o'er from fright," he declared seriously.

As they neared the carcass, Tate searched for a long limb, found one on a downed cottonwood, broke it off trimmed it up and started for the carcass. They used the pole to hang the carcass and with Hank on one end and Tate on the other, they carried the fresh meat back to camp. When they dropped the carcass near the wagon of Henry, Hank began excitedly telling his father the same story Tate had told about scaring the deer to death. The boy was tickled when his father looked at Tate in disbelief, until the boy told him the truth of the matter. His mother scolded him for telling "windys" and laughed with him as they cut fresh steaks for supper. The meat was shared among the rest of the families and everyone enjoyed the first fresh meat in several days.

CHAPTER SIX
BUFFALO

THE WAGON TRAIN HAD BEEN ON THE MOVE FOR ALMOST A week and Tate was pleased with the progress. Activity had become routine with good travel, although not without the challenges presented by the terrain, and each night's camp had fresh meat, either antelope or deer, and the people were in good spirits. Several had expressed their thanks to Tate for taking over from Bear. One woman had observed, "It just seems that everyone is so much happier since you've become our guide. Before, it seemed everyone was on edge all the time, even fearful of the next day, but it's so much better now. Thank you so much, Mr. Saint."

"It's Tate m'am, just Tate. But thank you for those kind words." He tipped his hat to the woman and quickly goaded his horse away from the wagon. He had off-loaded his gear from the pack-horses into a couple of the wagons and teth-ered the animals behind to avoid having to trail them on his scouts. After seeing a band of Indians on a far mesa, probably Sioux, he was wary of what they might run into and he wanted to move as surreptitiously as possible. If he could avoid being seen before he spotted any hostiles, he could give the wagons ample warning to defend themselves. The country they were traveling through was Cheyenne territory, but the Sioux and Crow were also known to hunt and raid in this area. Tate also knew these Indians were not used to seeing a wagon train and would be suspicious. Although they had seen trader caravans before, usually those bound for a rendezvous, the trade caravans never traveled with the prairie schooner type wagons and the white bonnets of these wagons would be a curiosity.

This day's travel had been a little more difficult than most with the trail scarred by several gullies and ravines that necessitated tough crossing with the steep sided ravines the most demanding. They topped out on a broad plateau with scattered patches of alkali. As they came to the far side of the flat-top, the trail dropped off the side and had been washed out, requiring they stop and using picks and shovels, fill in and smooth out the trail before passing. The hard work in the afternoon sun did little to mellow already soured temperaments, and the men grumbled as they climbed back aboard the wagons.

The river made a couple of sweeping curves, turning back on itself twice, and the trail was forced into the sand and clay hills that made the pulling harder on the teams. By the time the wagons dropped from the hills to the chosen campsite with scattered trees and along the river bank, the people were tired, dirty, and very relieved to call a halt to the day's travel. Although most were anxious to jump in the river and wash off the day's grime, they knew they had to tend to the stock first, and they wasted no time taking care of the animals. The usual routine was for the men to tend to the animals and gather wood for the fires while the women prepared the evening meal, but this day saw everyone hurrying to make it into the inviting water, even though it was somewhat murky.

Tate had taken a spot atop the bluff that overlooked the camp and was seated on a wide flat rock, elbows on knees and spyglass to his eye as he scanned the entire territory in every direction. While the laughter and jostling went on at the river, he searched for any sign of danger. His concern was if any raiding party of any of the tribes were to come upon the wagon train, they would be tempted to strike what might appear to be an easy target. Although Indians were not very interested in the long-eared mules, there were women, horses, and whatever secrets were hidden under the white bonnets of the wagons. A band of young bucks looking for honors and plunder might not be able to resist such temptation.

As he scanned the area, in the far distance to the northwest a dust cloud showed, just momentarily, but enough to cause concern. He knew it could be a herd of buffalo or a dust storm or even an Indian village on the move. If it was a village, he wasn't too concerned, because a raiding party or a hunting party would be careful not to show a dust cloud.

He continued scanning and another dust cloud showed, this one larger, closer and to the east north east and appeared to be coming this way. As he watched, he decided this was probably a herd of buffalo, too big a cloud for a village and moving too slow for a storm. He licked his lips at the thought of a fresh buffalo steak. He watched the cloud for a while, lifted his glass to the location of the other one farther away and seeing nothing, returned to look one last time at the nearer pillar of dust. As he scanned the terrain, he saw the natural contours and wide basin that seemed to show the herd would work their way to the river. At their present pace, they would arrive well after dark or even in the morning, just right for a good hunt. He made one last scan of the area all around and satisfied, put away the glass and started down the hillside.

While the others returned to their wagons and began the preparations for the evening meal, Tate did his bathing in a small spring fed stream back against the bluff and obscured in the alder and chokecherry bushes. When he was finished he donned a fresh set of buckskins, replacing the canvas britches and Linsey Woolsey shirt he had worn since Fort William. It felt good to be back in his customary garb and comfortable moccasins. He heard a voice hailing him and he stepped from behind the brush to see the twin daughters of the Bowmans, Cassandra and Charlotte, or as they preferred, Cassie and Charly, making their way up the slight slope to his camp. He greeted them with, "And just what are you two doing up here?" as he grinned at their approach.

Charly smiled and responded, "We wanted to invite you to our wagon for supper. Momma said to be sure to have you come cuz she's fixin' some berry pie, from those berries you showed us."

The girls were blossoming into womanhood and had caught the eyes of the two older boys, Mark and Jason, but the girls had avoided spending any time with the boys and didn't seem to be too interested in them. Now in the presence of Tate, they seemed to be acting a little more demurely than usual, but Tate thought nothing of it and replied, "Well, girls, that sounds just fine. I'll be glad to come to your wagon for supper. I've got a couple things to do 'fore I can come down, but you tell your folks I'll be along shortly. O.K.?"

Cassie smiled and said, "Don't keep us waiting too long now, y'hear?"

Tate chuckled and said, "Oh, I won't, I won't."

SYLVIA AND EDMOND BOWMAN had been sharecroppers on a farm in Missouri, and Edmond had served as the pastor of the small country church. Barely scraping by on the pittance of support given by the church and the small share of the crops of the farm owned by the head deacon of the church, the opportunity to have their own place and establish a mission work in the new territories seemed like an answer to prayer. Edmond was the cheerful sort, built somewhat like a straw filled scarecrow but not as gangly, while Sylvia would be described as portly. Red cheeks, button nose, curly light brown hair, and eyes that showed a bit of mischief made everyone happy to be in Sylvia's presence. Well known among the wagon train as an excellent cook, she had prepared a sumptuous spread for their guest.

"Good evening, folks. Your daughters extended an invitation and I'm hoping I wasn't mistaken," said Tate as he walked toward their wagon and the extended cover that shielded the dinner table.

"Oh, Mr. Saint, no, you were not mistaken, and we are pleased to have you join us," replied Edmond. "Please, have a seat," he added, motioning to the end of a bench beside the table. Tate doffed his hat and scooted onto the end of the bench, looking over the dishes of food. The boiled potatoes steamed, another bowl held prairie turnips and onions, and as he was seated, Mrs. Bowman sat a platter of smothered antelope steaks before him. But the fluffy biscuits and the bowl of gravy were what caught Tate's attention.

The smells brought a smile to Tate's face that was noted by Edmond, bringing a smile to his own. The girls were already seated and when Mrs. Bowman started to seat herself, both Tate and Edmond rose to acknowledge her presence and all were soon seated.

Edmond stretched his arms to the side, taking his wife's hand and the hand of Charly as he said, "Mr. Saint, we always ask the Lord's blessing before we eat, so if you'll join hands with us." Tate accepted the offered hand of Charly and reached across the table to take Cassie's hand and bowed his head. Edmond began, "Our heavenly Father, . . ." and continued with a short prayer of thanksgiving for the food and the company that soon ended with, "Amen." The others, including Tate, echoed the Amen and looked up to begin their meal.

Edmond dished up some potatoes, passed them and looked at Tate as he was placing some vegetables on his plate, and asked, "Mr. Saint,"

Tate interrupted him by saying, "Tate, please, just Tate."

"Yes, of course, Tate. Well, Tate, you didn't appear to be a stranger to the custom of praying before meals. Was that your habit as a boy at home?"

"Yes sir, still is," he replied, busy at forking a steak to his tin plate.

"Wonderful! So, you're a Christian then?" asked Edmond, prompting a scowl from Charly and Cassie.

"Well, sir. That depends on how you define Christian, now, doesn't it?" answered Tate as he began to eat, noticing the smile of the appreciated cook.

"Humm, yes, I suppose. Well, I would define a Christian as one who has come to that point in his life that he realized he was a sinner in need of a savior and chosen to accept the free gift of salvation as offered by Jesus Christ the Lord. Do you understand that, Tate?"

Tate looked at the man over his uplifted fork and said, "I understand. So, you wouldn't define a Christian as anyone that believes in God?"

"Oh no, the Bible says the devils believe and they tremble. So, when Jesus said a man must be born again to enter Heaven, He also explained in the book of Romans that the only way was to accept the gift of salvation, bought and paid for by Jesus on the cross," explained Edmond, starting to pontificate a bit.

Mrs. Bowman reached over and patted the back of

Edmond's hand and admonished him with, "Now dear, you promised to not start preaching."

He looked at his wife with a blank expression until he realized what she had said and was immediately aware of the stares from his wife and daughters. He dropped his eyes to the table and spoke in an apologetic tone, "I apologize Tate. I'm afraid my wife is right, I do get carried away rather easily. It's just that I'm concerned about others and, well, I, uh . . ."

Tate grinned at the man's embarrassment and said, "That's quite alright, Mr. Bowman. I could never be offended by anyone that was concerned about my salvation. But let me assure you, I have accepted Christ as my Savior and I know that Heaven is my home."

Tate's reply elated his host and his response of lifting his head with a broad smile and a bit of a chuckle gave everyone else a sense of relief that was shown by their smiles. Mrs. Bowman, wanting to change the direction of the conversation, asked, "So, is your meal acceptable, Tate?"

"Why, yes m'am. It's very good. Your reputation as the best cook on the train is well-deserved," he replied, bringing a smile to Mrs. Bowman.

The rest of the mealtime was filled with comments about farm life in Missouri and life as a pastor and family. But when the questions were directed to Tate, he shared very little about his life, speaking mostly about his youth with his teacher father and helpful mother. The girls tried to learn more, but he answered in general if not evasive terms and instead shared knowledge about the animals and wilderness.

As Tate prepared to leave he asked Edmond, "Sir, of those on the train, who would you say is the best hunter or best shot with a rifle?"

Edmond looked at Tate with a slightly wrinkled brow that showed both surprise and curiosity as he thought for a minute then answered, "Well, I would say Lucas Colgan, the big blacksmith, and Matthew Webster, Mark's father, and let's see, uh, probably Charles Heaton." He looked at Tate, wondering, as he asked, "And just why are you asking about those that are handy with a rifle?" He watched Tate's expression and had a sudden thought. He lowered his voice and asked, "You're not expecting an Indian attack, are you?"

Tate drew back as he looked at the man, then let a grin tug at his mouth as he answered, "No, no, not an Indian attack," yet as he said it, he thought of the other dust cloud, knowing it could be an Indian village on the move. He explained with, "But there is a possibility of running into some buffalo."

CHAPTER SEVEN
HUNT

LOBO NUDGED TATE AWAKE AND BEGAN PACING AROUND THE man, excited and nervous, looking to the bluff, anxious for Tate to follow. The position of the moon showed it was early morning, well before dawn and the clear night was littered with stars. Tate warily slipped from his blankets, but as he watched Lobo, he knew there was no danger, but the wolf wanted Tate to follow. At the man's signal, the wolf trotted up the slight trail that led to the top of the mesa where he had surveyed the countryside the day before. As Tate neared the crest of the bluff, he heard and even felt the low thunder of the moving herd of buffalo. Once atop the plateau, he walked to the far edge and looked at the wide shadow moving down the broad valley toward the river. The moonlight showed the rising dust cloud that followed the herd as the wooly beasts moved as one rolling blanket of darkness.

He watched as the herd approached the river, slowing their progress and crowding the bank, many pushed into the water as they slaked their thirst after the long dusty trek. As they settled down, the noise of the bellows and rattling of horns began to subside and many of the animals moved away searching for graze. The herd covered an area of about 20 acres and Tate estimated it to be less than a thousand animals. He had taken note of the wide plains and the abundance of buffalo grass on the preceding day and knew the animals, if left undisturbed, would stay in the valley for a few days. It was not unusual for a herd of this size to be undisturbed even by a few rifle shots, as long as there was nothing more alarming that appeared as a threat to the whole herd. It was this lack of fear, because they were such massive beasts and had few predators, that enabled some buffalo hunters to take great numbers, often as many as a hundred, before the herd would move away from their graze. Packs of wolves often followed the herds in their migrations but were only a threat to the weak or old animals, seldom able to take a young calf because of the protective mothers. They were often seen serving as the clean-up crew after the passing of the herd.

Tate lingered in his moonlight observation of the buffalo until the thin band of grey painted the eastern horizon to warn of coming sunlight. He took one last look at the herd, affirming his plan for the hunt, and with Lobo at his side moved back to his campsite. He saddled Shady and led the horse toward the camp of the wagons, Lobo now leading the way. The people were stirring, some starting their cooking fires and others going to the bushes for their morning constitutional, as Tate moved to the wagon of Lucas Colgan.

The big man was stirring the coals of the previous night's fire when he looked up to see Tate approaching and greeted him with, "Mornin'," and continued building the fire.

"Mornin' Lucas. Say, would you be interested in a chance at takin' a buffalo?" asked Tate.

The big man, scooting forward on his seat, looked wide-eyed and anxious at his visitor and answered, "Why sure! I'd like to try to take a buffalo. I hear they're mighty good eatin'!"

"That they are. Saddle up and meet me by the river soon's your ready. I'm gonna see if a couple others'd like to come along." Tate waved over his shoulder as he walked toward the other wagons. Within just a few moments, his invitations to Matt Webster and Charles Heaton had been gladly accepted and all four men were soon gathered at the riverside. Tate grinned at the obvious excitement of the men and began to explain what he expected them to do on the hunt. He motioned toward the edge of the finger bluff that draped from the nearby mesa toward the river and said, "They're just on the other side of that bluff yonder, but I'm thinkin' it'd be best if we cross over the river here, move upstream a ways and then cross back over under cover of the willows an' stuff. We can take positions at the edge of the brush and do our shootin' from there. Now, we don't need more'n two or three, four at the most. That'd be 'nuff meat to last the whole train some time, so, don't think ya' gotta be doin' a lot'a shootin'." He chuckled a bit and added, "After you hafta dress a buffler out, you'll not be too anxious to shoot too many. That's a lot o' hard work, I'm sayin'."

Each of the men nodded their understanding and Tate gigged his horse to the water to start their crossing. The water was no more than belly deep on the horses and the crossing was easy and made in moments. They moved upstream about a half mile and Tate motioned for them to cross back to the north side of the river. Once out of the water, Tate slipped to the ground, located a grassy patch and stretched a rope between a couple of cottonwoods to picket the horses. He went to the men, looking at their rifles and noticed the one held by Matt Webster, a Kentucky style flint-lock, appeared to be of smaller caliber. He looked at the man and asked, "Just how big is that?" motioning to the rifle.

Matt quickly answered, "Why, it's .38 caliber. I've taken many deer with this rifle, accurate to, oh, 'bout, a hundred yards." They were speaking in low voices, not wanting to stir the herd.

Tate looked at the others, who held the muzzles toward him and then back to Matt and said, "That might be alright for a deer, but I doubt if it'd punch a hole in the hide of a buffalo. Tell ya' what, how 'bout you take my Hawken." Tate extended the rifle toward him and cautioned, "Now, that's loaded for buffalo and it'll kick a mite, but it can drop a buffler, if you hit it right, that is." He slipped his powder horn and possibles bag over his shoulder and added, "There's patches and balls in the bag there, an' the powder measure is the little horn tip there, fill it up to the brim. Caps is in the bag too."

"Well, thanks Tate, but what will you use?" asked Webster, eyes lifted in question to their guide.

"Oh, don't worry 'bout me," he explained, and turned to the others as he began to give additional instructions. "Now, the best place to hit 'em is a heart shot, low chest, behind the front leg as you know. The best eatin' will be a cow, but don't take one with a calf alongside. Or, a take a young bull, but avoid them big'uns. All you'll do is make 'em mad and their tougher'n boot leather anyway. Make sure your target is sorta by themselves and you won't spook the herd too bad. But be sure to reload right away. The last thing you want is a mad buffalo chargin' and you with an empty rifle."

The men waited while Tate retrieved his longbow and quiver and watched while he strung it, preparing for the hunt. He led the way into the brush, positioned the men and said in a whisper, "Wait till everyone's ready. I'll give the signal." Within moments the shooters were ready and Tate, looking from one to the other said just above a whisper, "Take your shots!" The sudden barrage of rifle fire made the entire herd tense and they lurched as one, but they did not move away, just looked for the source of the noise. The men had scored with their shots. Webster using Tate's Hawken had scored a perfect hit on his chosen animal, and the cow moved just two steps and crumpled in place. Lucas, using a .54 caliber percussion Kentucky, also dropped his young bull with a perfect heart shot. Charles Heaton had an unusually large bore, .60 caliber flintlock, loaded for bear, and hit his cow in the shoulder, bringing the animal down, but not killing it.

Suddenly the valley was cut with screams and yells as a horde of Indians attacked the herd from the far flank. The buffalo rose as one and started at a run to escape this sudden and frightening attack. The ground shook and the thunder raised as bellowing buffalo moved as a stampeding horde, shaking the very earth where the men stood. Tate jumped atop a downed log, stretching as high as possible to try to see through the quickly rising dust cloud, but he knew these attackers were from the Indian village he thought he'd seen the day before.

As the herd thundered past, the men with Tate were shocked to feel the solid earth beneath them tremble with the rumble of a volcano as the massive beasts beat the staccato rhythm of hoof on soil in their panicked flight. The men rose to their feet and edged nearer their guide, fearful of the phenomenon of the herd and the dread of a possible Indian attack.

Lucas asked, "Who are they?"

"Dunno, too far to see, but I'm hopin' they're Cheyenne," answered Tate. "Reload anyway!" he commanded. The men, suddenly realizing they were holding empty rifles, hurriedly began the task of reloading, nervously looking up as often as possible to see if the Indians were coming their direction. Tate stood with the bow, arrow nocked, at his side as he continued to watch the action before him. As he looked at the passing animals, he saw a lazy cow moving apart from the herd and he pulled up his bow, stepped into it and released the arrow to its target. The men were surprised to see the arrow fly true and the cow stumble like a drunken sailor for several steps before finally falling over on her side, legs kicking as she bled out. When the men looked back at Tate, they were surprised to see him with another arrow nocked and the man taking aim at another buffalo. Again, he fired and again the target, a young bull, was impaled but continued trotting, the feathered arrow flopping like a flag, but after no more than ten yards, the bull's head dropped, and he plowed a furrow with his snout before upending and flipping over to land with a thud, dead. As the men turned to looked back at Tate, he had another arrow nocked, but the bow was held at his side.

Tate looked at Heaton and said, "When you approach that cow, be careful. I think you broke its shoulder, but she ain't dead. So, be ready to put another ball into her. She can get up and charge even with three legs." The man nodded and looked at the downed animal as it continued to struggle to get up. The herd had moved away and left behind nothing but the downed animals and a thick cloud of dust and Tate spoke to all the men and said, "Go 'head on and start your butcherin'. I'm gonna go see our neighbors, so, wish me luck."

CHAPTER EIGHT
CHEYENNE

TATE UNSTRUNG HIS BOW, SLIPPED IT INTO ITS SHEATH, PUT HIS Hawken in the scabbard and mounted up. He told the men, "Now, go 'head and start your butcherin' but keep your rifles handy and stay alert. If them Injuns come chargin' in you hightail it back 'cross the river n'get to the wagons and sound the alarm. But, I'm hopin' they're Cheyenne and friendly. If they are, we'll be safe enough."

"Well, you be careful, cuz without you we'd be left high n' dry out here with none of us knowin' where ta' go!" warned Heaton as the other men nodded their heads in agreement.

"Ah, ain't no big secret. All ya' gotta do is foller the Platte yonder to the Sweetwater. Then follow that to South Pass, an' just keep on going till ya' get to Oregon. Simple 'nuff. But, ain't nothin' gonna happen to my momma's little boy, so don't be worryin' none." He chuckled as he pointed Shady across the churned-up passage of the buffalo and Lobo trotted alongside.

A SHORT WHILE LATER, he saw a few carcasses, arrows

protruding like quills from a porcupine, and he stopped to await the return of the hunters. As he sat, leaning on the pommel of his saddle, he looked back the direction of the herd's line of travel and saw the approach of the rest of the Indian village, women leading horses with travois, children and dogs running, and a few older men and women following along. It was a good-sized group of people and Tate knew they had probably already set up their village back in the draw in a protected setting with both terrain and trees to shield it from view. They now moved with empty travois to gather the meat. Tate looked back toward the direction where the herd stampeded and saw the hunters returning.

They were a jovial bunch, laughing and jostling together as they bragged about their success and kidded others about their stories. When the leader saw Tate, he reined up and the rest of the hunters stopped behind him, watching the white man before them. Tate could tell they were speaking in low voices to one another and the leader raised his hand for them to stay where they were as he moved towards their visitor. When he approached Tate, he lifted his hand in a peaceful gesture, palm forward and open.

Tate slowly raised his hand in a similar motion and waited for the leader to approach. As he came near, Tate saw him searching not only his face for any sign of danger, but his belongings as well. The Indian's eyes lingered on Lobo, standing beside Shady, and back at Tate, obviously wondering at this man with a wolf at his side. Tate had purposely let his quiver hang from the saddle horn and the longbow extended beyond the end of the sheath. He watched as the man looked at the gear, up at Tate and back at the weapons. He spoke in Cheyenne and said as he motioned to himself, "Tsétsėhéstáhese, Cheyenne."

Tate grinned and replied in Arapaho, "Good, I was hopin'

you were Cheyenne. I am Longbow, friend of the Arapaho and Cheyenne."

The Indian looked at Tate, and Tate wondered if he had understood. The man looked again at the quiver and the end of the longbow and spoke in English, "You are Longbow?"

Tate nodded and said, "Yes, I am Longbow, and what are you called?"

"I am Aénohe Óhvó'komaestse, White Hawk." He motioned to the other hunters and added, "We are Dog Soldiers of the Só'taétaneo'o. These," motioning to the approaching women and others, "are our people."

Tate looked back at the women and turned to look at White Hawk and said, "White Hawk, when we saw your people start your hunt, I wanted to give a gift to your people to thank you for sharing your hunt with us. I have taken two buffalo as a gift to your people. If you will accept them, I will take you to them."

Tate watched as the man studied him and waited for his response. Tate knew this was an unusual action for a white man and he watched as White Hawk tried to see if any deceit shown in eyes. He was relieved when the leader of the Indians lifted his head slightly and motioned for Tate to lead the way. As Tate reined around, he saw White Hawk motion for some of the others to follow as well.

When the other men, busy at their butchering, saw Tate approaching with the four Indians, they each stood, making sure their rifles were within reach, cautiously watching as the small group of Indians with Tate drew near. Tate stopped at the carcass of the young bull and slid from his saddle, and motioning to the Indians, was joined by White Hawk and his men. Hawk noticed the arrow protruding from the bull and looked to the white man and asked, "You took him with your longbow? Were you mounted?"

Tate replied, "No, I wasn't mounted. That bow is not good

from horseback. I was over yonder by the willows," nodding his head toward the riverbank and the clusters of brush that were just shy of a hundred yards off. As White Hawk looked, Tate knew he was mentally calculating the distance and he grinned as the Indian shook his head in disbelief.

He asked, "You came closer, yes?"

"No," he replied simply, and knelt to split the buffalo open from neck to tail. As the guts spilled out, the steam rose, and Tate reached in to get the liver, cut it free and split the bladder to access the bile. He handed the liver to White Hawk, which was an honor, and Hawk dipped the tip of the liver in the bile, put the tip in his teeth and with a quick slice of his knife in front of his nose, cut the bit free and began chewing as he handed the liver back to Tate. Tate mimicked the action of Hawk then handed the liver to one of the other warriors and watched as they copied. Tate had motioned his men to join them and when the last Indian had his bite, he handed it to Lucas. The big man looked at Tate with a wide-eyed expression and Tate motioned for him to follow suit. All the men, though rather timidly, did as the others and all eight men were soon grinning and laughing, blood trailing from their mouths and hands.

Hawk looked up at the big blacksmith who stood almost a head taller than anyone else and easily weighed at least fifty pounds more, and Hawk asked, "Did you take a buffalo?"

"Yes, first one too," proudly proclaimed the big man.

Hawk asked as he pantomimed for clarity, "Did you hit it," motioning with a fist suggesting the big man could knock out a buffalo with his fist, "or did you shoot it?" mimicking a rifle shot.

His expression was serious, and Lucas looked to Tate, saw his wide grin and realized the Indian was funning him. Lucas formed a very sober expression and said, "I had to shoot him. He was running too fast for me to catch!" He also pantomimed with exaggerated motions, much to the laughter of everyone, even the other Indians.

Hawk looked to Tate and said, "We should feast. Bring your people and join us." He motioned to the wide grassy flat near the river and said, "There, as sun sets. Yes?"

Tate nodded and said, "Yes, we would be honored."

As Hawk and his men rode away, the men from the wagons looked at Tate and Lucas asked, "Are we really gonna have a feast with 'em?"

"Why not? They're good people and your folks'd probably like meetin' some real wild Indians. They might surprise you, they are pretty good cooks."

"Well, at least we'll have plenty of meat to eat," declared Heaton as he started back to the carcass to finish his work. The others went to their butchering and Tate said, "I'm gonna go tell the rest of the folks about the party so they can do whatever they need to do." The men waved as Tate mounted up to return to the wagons and they returned to the bloody work of butchering.

When Tate rode in among the wagons, he called everyone near and announced, "Folks, we've been invited to a good ol' fashioned potluck dinner!"

Smiles spread around the group as they looked at one another until Henry Hyde asked, "Well, who is it? Another wagon train?"

Tate chuckled, anticipating a shocked response and said, "Nope, it's our neighbors, the Cheyenne!"

The crowd's smiles turned to shock, and they looked at one another, and back at Tate as Henry asked, "You can't be serious? Indians have asked us to a dinner? I ain't never heard of such a thing!"

Tate leaned forward with his forearms on his pommel and said, "Folks, I know it's unusual, but the Cheyenne have long been peaceable with whites and we just shared a buffalo hunt. Oh and by the way, your men have three downed buffalo they're butcherin' on right now, and when the Cheyenne came around, they invited us to join in the customary feast after a successful hunt. So, we can all join 'em, just past that bluff yonder, o'er near the river, and have a good old-fashioned picnic 'bout sundown."

As the farmer families chattered among themselves, they moved back toward their wagons, as a few remained behind with questions for Tate. He stepped down from Shady, Lobo at his side and began to field the questions, explaining what they could expect and should do, he finished with, "We'll take a couple wagons so we can haul the meat back, an' folks'll ride together and we should have a real good time. I think you'll find the only difference will be just that they wear a few less clothes than we do, but otherwise they get hungry just like us."

It was an eager though slightly nervous group that rode in the wagons or rode their horses alongside. When they rounded the point of the bluff and saw the beginnings of a village with several tipis already up and children playing and cookfires burning, they began to relax at the sight of families enjoying themselves.

When the villagers saw the approaching wagons, most stopped what they were doing and looked at the many whites drawing near. It was just as surprising to the Cheyenne as it was to the whites that this feast would be a joint affair. But once they saw the women and children, the Cheyenne women resumed their work at the fires. Several were finishing the butchering in the field and would join them shortly.

Tate had already explained that most of the communication would have to be with hand signs but there might be a few that could speak English. He had explained the tradition of the Indian that the women would serve the men and eat separately, and it would probably be best if they did the same. When the women looked at one another, Tate could tell they questioned what he was saying, but they were willing to follow his guidance. He was cautioned not to try to make it a habit though, the caution coming from the wagon driving Gertrude, to the laughter of the other women.

EVERYONE, at first, kept to themselves. The Indian women stayed by the fires, sneaking an occasional glance at the whites, while the white women busied themselves laying out their prepared dishes on the improvised tables, also stealing a look at the Indians as opportunity presented. Gertrude led an entourage of women from the wagons, carrying pots and pans needing room at the fire and as they approached the ladies in buckskin, they were greeted by one woman who introduced herself in English as Dove that Talks. When Gertrude made their needs known, Dove ushered the ladies to the cookfires, translating for each one and introducing them to one another. Before long the women were sharing and by use of signs and motions, made themselves understood and the barriers of suspicion and fear slowly fell.

White Hawk had assembled the men in the center of the gathering where an assortment of blankets had been provided for everyone to be seated. The Indians were accustomed to being seated in a circle, with the important leaders at the head, and those of lesser status farther around the circle. The whites simply moved around the outside of the circle, interspersed with several of the warriors. White Hawk had Tate sit to his right with a rather imposing man to his left, who was introduced as Big Horn, their shaman. Suitable for his name he was adorned in a skull top of a buffalo with both horns and the cape hanging down the back of his neck.

Tate noticed the man never changed his stoic expression throughout the evening.

Soon the women began serving the men and all were surprised when the white women bore full plates or wooden platters to the Indian men and the white men were served by the Indian women. White Hawk looked to a particular server, lifting his shoulders and extending his hands to ask a question, but was waved off by the woman, who, he explained to Tate, was his woman or wife, Dove that Talks. Tate chuckled at the exasperated expression on the leader and said, "I guess the women have kind of taken over. You might regret this little feast, chief."

"These white women are, uh, strong spirit," he said, somewhat confounded.

Tate laughed at his expression and answered, "Yeah, they are, that's why I took a wife of the Arapaho."

White Hawk looked at Tate, surprise showing in his eyes, "You have a woman of the Arapaho?"

"Had, she's crossed over. But she was a fine woman," he remarked wistfully.

As the mealtime waned, Tate saw the two groups intermingling as if they were one. Hank, the son of Henry Hyde and the boy that had often followed Tate around like a puppy, had found a friend and the two were playing a common hoop game of the Cheyenne. The Bowman sisters were walking with two Indian girls of about the same age, followed closely by Mark Hillyard and Jason Pickett who had been seen earlier talking with a couple of young warriors of the Cheyenne. The women were working together as they cleaned up after the meal and were almost comical in their antics as they sought to make each other understand.

When the plates and platters had been cleared, White Hawk brought out a long stemmed carved red soapstone pipe and motioned to Tate for him to join. Tate said, "I'd be honored, but wouldn't it be more appropriate for some of my men to join our circle?"

"Yes, that would be good," replied White Hawk and he stood to speak to several of his people seated in the circle. At his direction, several stood up, making room for others and White Hawk said, "You have your men to join the circle, there," motioning to the standing men.

Tate stood and called out to his men and asked, "How 'bout five of you fellas take a seat alongside those that are standing?" The men of the wagons looked at one another and with Lucas Colgan, the big blacksmith, leading, four others followed to join the circle. Matt Webster and Charles Heaton, the hunters with Lucas, and Henry Hyde and Jeffrey Pickett seated themselves among the Cheyenne.

White Hawk filled the pipe, used a firebrand to light it, then lifting it toward the four directions, to the Heavens and to the Earth, he took a long puff, exhaled and handed the pipe to Tate. Tate repeated the actions and passed the pipe, as did all the others in the circle. When the pipe completed its circuit, White Hawk laid it aside and stood to speak.

"It has been good to feast with our friends," and he looked at Tate and continued, "and you my friend have shown us honor with your gift of buffalo." He reached behind him to receive a bundle from a waiting warrior, turned back to Tate and said, "May this always show our friendship for as long as the sun passes over." He handed the package to Tate and continued, "All of you," and made a sweeping motion to indicate all the visiting whites including the women that had gathered on the outer edge of the crowd, "have given us your friendship and we have given ours. May Ma'heo'o, the Sacred Being, give His blessing on all that are here."

The short talk of the chief signified the end of the festivities and everyone started their return to their camps. As the crowd dispersed, White Hawk motioned to Tate to join him and the two men returned to their seats, Tate waiting for White Hawk to speak. The chief paused and looked at his new friend and began, "My scouts have known of your wagons for many days. They also tell me of others that follow you."

Tate immediately thought of Bear and his crew from Fort William, thinking it was probably the disgruntled trapper and his followers that shadowed the wagon train. He looked at White Hawk, realizing the man had more to say and waited.

"That group has white men in buckskins, one very big man with face hair," he motioned with his hands indicating a big beard. "There are also outcasts, or what you would call renegades. Men of other tribes that have been sent away from their people. Some were Lakota, some Crow, mebbe from the Comanche and Kiowa. Others join them."

Tate knew he was referring to the renegades that were rejected by their own people and always seemed to find others that were just as vile and evil, yet still sought like-minded company. He looked at White Hawk and asked, "Did your scouts say how many there were?"

"Two hands, maybe more," he replied. "These are bad men, even their own people hate them. They have been sent from the villages because they refuse the traditions of their people. Some have killed their own people and do not honor Ma'heo'o. Our God has turned his back on them. My scouts believe they follow you to attack. You must prepare for that. If they attack you when you are near, we will fight with you."

Tate was surprised at Hawk's offer to join the fight and replied, "You do us great honor to be ready to fight with us. But, we don't know if or when they mean to attack. We will try to be away from your territory before that." Tate stood to leave and clasped forearms with his friend as he bid him goodbye. As he walked back to the wagons to join the others

on their return to their camp, he thought about the renegades, and he didn't like the odds of ten vicious and fearless
warriors against their maybe twelve rifles, and several of
those having never taken anything bigger than a squirrel or
at best a little whitetail deer.

When the wagons pulled back into the circle of their
camp, everyone clambered down, and the men started
unloading the bounty of buffalo meat. Tate suggested they
hang the meat in the trees near the stream and said they
would smoke some tomorrow. The people were surprised
they would have another day of rest, but no one complained.
It had been an unusual and memorable day, but all were
looking forward to turning in for the night.

CHAPTER NINE

BEAR STRUGGLED TO FIND A COMFORTABLE POSITION, PUSHING himself against the tree, stretching out his injured leg. Grumbling and grunting all the while, the big man growled at his long-time partner, Gramps, "Grab me some o' dat meat!" as he motioned to the deer steaks hanging over the fire. The older man, called Gramps because of his prematurely gray hair and surly disposition, snatched up a willow stick with a dripping steak and stretched out to hand it to the gruff self-appointed leader of the group. The big man was called Bear because everything about him made one think of a bear. His thick black whiskers that hid whatever neck he had and hung over his chest, his size that was the equivalent of a large black bear, and even his unwashed smell like that of a long hibernating bruin. His stench spoke of his lineage that he bragged was from the biggest bear in the woods.

Gramps' head was topped with a thick patch of gray, almost white hair that hung down his neck and shoulders that made him look like a seeding milkweed caught in a windstorm. Where Bear was dark and dirty, Gramps was pink skinned and fastidious. No two more opposite men could be found, except in their disposition.

The third man in the crew was called Gimpy, because of a club foot that gave him a considerable limp. His disposition was almost the match of Bear's, and he was always grumbling and complaining, blaming everyone and everything for his condition. He was quick to anger, eager to kill and was given every dirty job the crew undertook. He was skilled as a sneak-thief and pickpocket, often using his disability to distract his target from the deed.

Hoots was a half-breed, with a Crow father and captive white mother. His Crow name was Owl that Walks, and with the owl being an omen of death or disaster among the Indians, it was easy to understand his isolation and rejection. Yet before he earned his warrior name, he was known as Red Fox and had exceeded his peers with his skills with a bow and at tracking. But his behavior toward women and his prowling in the night earned him his name of disdain and subsequent banishment from the village.

Evil always finds company and this group of four began with Bear and Gramps. The others were added as they found each other's company during some drunken brawl. Bear, by his sheer size, was their leader, although they hadn't been together but a couple of months when Bear had taken on the role of guide for the wagons. Before he left St. Joseph with the farmers, he sent Gimpy and Hoots ahead to scout out a location for their takeover. But during the stretch of the trail from St. Joseph to Fort William, after finding they had both a considerable amount of good supplies and money as well, he decided to milk the wagon train for all he could, it was an easy job and a good way to make it back to the mountains. But when the people of the wagons replaced him with that young pup, his blood boiled with a desire for vengeance.

Bear knew his leg wasn't broken, but that kick on the side

of his knee damaged it somehow and it wouldn't hold his weight. After having to watch the wagons pull out without him, and not getting the extra money he believed was due, he had been plotting and scheming of some way to get what he thought was owed him and everything else from those pilgrims. As he bit into the steak, juices streaming into his beard, he growled at Hoots, "Kin you git any o' yore Injun friends to join up wit us? You know, other'ns like you that wuz kicked out an' are madder'n an' ol' wet hornet an' willin' to do anything?"

Hoots lifted his face from his gnawing on the meat and answered, "Yuh, prob'ly. There's other'ns like me all o'er. Some of 'ems hooked up together'n doin' what'er it takes to git by."

"Wal, wha'dya hafta do ta' find 'em?"

"They be there," pointing to the West and the long range of mountains, "still holding snow on top, sometimes referred to as the Laramie mountains, mebbe north in Bighorns by Medicine Wheel," explained Hoots.

"Medicine Wheel, whassat?" taunted Bear.

"Place of Spirits, north in mountains."

"How many ya' reckon ya' can git?" growled Bear, leaning to get another steak from Gramps.

Hoots leaned back and looked at the big man and answered, "This many," holding up one hand, fingers outstretched, "mebbe this many," holding up both hands, indicating ten.

"I'm thinkin' I'd like to have more'n that. Whatta bout'chur tribe, think ya can get any from there?" snarled Bear, talking around his chewing.

Hoots shrugged his shoulders as an answer, then said, "Mebbe."

The others knew when Bear started asking questions it was because he was planning something, and they scooted closer to the big man to hear what was on his mind. He didn't disappoint as he began, "Here's whut I'm thinkin' on. I know them pilgrims had a bunch more money than they wus lettin' on, cuz they'd be needin' to buy more 'quipment 'n seed 'n such. They shore wasn't haulin' 'nuff wit' 'em and they up 'n offered that snot nosed punk cash up front, so I knows they got it. Now, I aim for us to be gettin' it an' anything else that suits our fancy. And I aim to teach that kid whut for, too. So, Hoots," and he pointed at the half-breed, "I want you ta' go roundup all them other renegades you can find, tell 'em that wagon trains got gold an' women an' guns, that'll get thar interest, shore 'nuff." Bear scooted forward on his haunches, wincing at the pain in his leg and turned to Gramps and said, "Now, Gramps, I want you ta' kinda search out this place, y'know, the store an' that poor excuse for a tavern an see if'n you cain't get us 'nother man or two or so." He looked at Gimpy and said, "I want you ta' get us pack-horse or two, prob'ly from some o' these Injuns 'round here, an' we'll get us some supplies fer this little adven'chur. Oh, an' when yore bickerin' fer them pack-horses, see if you can get one or two o' them bucks to come wit' us, you know, give 'em some whiskey an' promises."

Bear snatched at the last hanging steak and as he slipped it from the willow he looked at the three and said, "When we hit them wagons, I mean ta' take ever'thing! I mean ever last thing an' I especially mean them snippy girls that pranced aroun' all the time. We'll let them renegade Injuns have ever'thing but the money an' them two girls, and they'll make it look like twern't nuthin' but Injuns done it. You know how they do, what with mutilatin' ever' man an' woman, after they get done with 'em. An' if we do it right, we might just set ourselves up to take some o' them ronny'vous traders, or mebbe some o' them whut's been goin' down Sante Fe way." He chomped down on the meat, cackled at the thought of future attacks and nodded his head at the others as he asked, "Don't that sound good?" Not waiting for any response, he answered his own question, "Yessiree it do, it sounds mighty good!" He looked at his men, scowled and growled, "Now, go on an' get to it! You got yore jobs, go on, scram!"

CHAPTER TEN
PLANNING

TATE TOOK HIS VIGIL ATOP THE MESA BEFORE FIRST LIGHT. With the coming of the dawn, he searched the terrain, focusing on the broad plains of the east, knowing the rolling hills could hide thousands of pursuers. If the band of renegades, probably led by Bear, was following them, he hoped to get a glimpse of them or at least their dust as they began to move, before they expected anyone to be watching.

As the rising sun painted the desolate plain with its elusive gold, shadows retreated, and the flats began to move with life. Antelope stirred as some stood and stretched, cacti opened their blossoms to catch the morning sun, rabbits stood tall on hind feet surveying their domain, coyotes scratched at fleas behind their ears, and overhead a broad winged eagle began his search for breakfast. Tate always enjoyed seeing the day come to life, and he was relieved when the only living moving things he saw had four legs. He shimmied back from his flat-rock promontory, retreated in a crouch and moved down the trail to his camp at the foot of the bluff.

The people of the wagons were stirring, men gathering

firewood, women preparing the first meal of the day, kids looking for mischief and some of the young people tasked with taking the horses to water. The morning light sought to bend its bands of gold over the mesa to reach the camp, the bright rays bringing an almost blinding brilliance into the busy camp. Tate had saddled the grulla while a lazy Lobo watched and soon the threesome was walking toward the wagons, readying for the day's journey.

Tate motioned to the men as he passed their wagons and he headed to the side of Henry Hyde, to await the others to join them. He looked over the group, saw all the men present and drew them away from the wagon, out of earshot of the women, before he gave them the news. "The last thing White Hawk told me last night was about somethin' his scouts had been watchin'. Seems we got some folks that 'pear to be followin' us."

He was immediately interrupted by the nervous Russell Prescott, "Following us? Who's following us? More Injuns?"

A general sense of alarm was shown by the movement of the men, some looking back toward the wagons, others beyond. Tate raised his hands and said, "Now, hold on, hold on. What he said was that there were some white men, his words were white men in buckskins,"

Again the obviously frightened Prescott interrupted, "Why are they followin' us?" he blurted.

Lucas leaned over and slightly bumped Prescott and said, "Well, mebbe if you'd listen, he might tell us." The chastised man looked up at the big blacksmith, then dropped his head and nodded.

Tate continued, "These white men in buckskins were led by a big man with a big black beard." He paused for just a moment to watch the reaction of the men as they quickly realized that the bearded man had to be none other than their discharged guide, Bear.

"But that ain't all, White Hawk's scouts say he's gatherin' up some renegades, outcasts from some o' the tribes. These are Indians that their own tribes have kicked out for one reason or another. Usually, they're purty rotten types."

"Well, what're they after?" asked Heaton.

"Ever'thing," answered Tate, giving the men a moment to allow that thought to take root.

"What can we do?" asked Jeffrey Pickett, his wife was the wagon driver and his boy, Jason, was interested in one of the twin girls. Jeffrey had been a pretty quiet man, probably because his wife seldom gave him an opportunity to express himself. His response was not like the nervous Prescott, more of a man that had been told of a problem and he was ready to apply the solution, whatever it might be, he stood ready.

"Fight," answered Tate.

"But, but, how many are there and where, uh, how, uh, what do you mean, fight?" queried the nervous Prescott. Lucas scowled at him again, and the man mumbled, "Well, I'm, uh, concerned," as he looked up at the big man.

The rest of the men looked to Tate, anxious for his response, and he began, "Well, first, I wanted you all to know and give you a chance to think about it and make sure you're ready. I suggest you, in your own way and own time, tell your women folks, even the kids, about what we're facing. And, I expect you to make sure you all don't do anythin' foolish, like wanderin' away from the wagons or nuthin'." He saw nodding heads and expectant faces, then he took a deep breath and added, "We'll keep movin' today, you men keep your rifles at the ready, and when we stop this evenin', we'll get back together and talk it out and with all of us thinkin' 'bout it, I'm sure we'll come up with a good plan. Now, who's in the lead wagon today?"

Felix Robidoux raised his hand and Tate addressed him,

"Alright Felix, I think you'll find the road easy 'nuff to follow, it purty well sidles along the river an' it'll be up to you to pick the spot for the noonin'." Tate turned to the group and said, "Now Mr. Pickett, I need your boy, Jason, and Mr. Hillyard, I need your boy, Mark. Now, both them boys have shown themselves purty good horsemen and not bad shots. So, I need them both armed and mounted. I'm gonna have them scoutin' ahead, while I hang back to try to get an idea 'bout them that's follerin' us."

The men returned to their wagons and the harnessing of the mules, with the few days of not traveling, the mules were a little more stubborn but soon were rigged and ready. Tate saw the two young men riding towards him and he swung aboard the grulla and motioned for the two to follow. Lobo trotted alongside, taking his cue from the movement of the horse. Tate reined up and turned to look at the two newly recruited scouts and started instructing them in their duties, finishing with, "Now, don't go shootin' at the first thing you see. If its an Indian, he might be a friendly Cheyenne an' we don't wanna be startin' no Injun wars. Best thing you can do is try to make yourself as invisible as possible, stay in the cover, don't skyline yourselves, and always be aware of what's around you. Now, ever so often, one of you drop off to the side and check out the flank, but always keep one of you out front. Don't go shootin' any game, we've got enough buffalo to last a while an' we don't wanna be tellin' anyone where we are by shootin'." The boys had sat attentive and nodded their heads as they understood, yet they were excited about this man-sized opportunity. "If you see any danger, don't try to meet it head-on, your responsibility is to the rest of the folks so you need to be warnin' 'em, understand?"

The two young men answered in unison, "Yessir!"

Tate grinned and said, "I know you'll do a good job, just don't forget, we're all countin' on you."

"Where you gonna be, Tate?" asked Mark.

"I'm gonna be checkin' out our back-trail, see who might be followin' us.

"We'll do it, you can count on us. Can't he, Mark?" said Jason, looking to his friend. Both nodded as they looked to Tate.

They were answered with, "I know you'll do fine, fellas."

Felix Robidoux with his wife Angelique at his side, uncoiled his bullwhip and cracked it above the heads of his lead mules and the grey beasts leaned into their traces, pulling the trace chains taut with a rattle and the creak of wheels that had settled into the soil. As soon as the wagon moved, those behind made their own protests with creaking, rattling, and even one disgruntled mule baring his teeth and braying his protest. But within moments, all wagons were on the move and Tate sat astride Shady with Lobo belly down beside him, watching the prairie schooners set sail on another day's trek. When they passed his station, Tate reined his mount around and started up the adobe bluff, Lobo alongside, to begin his reconnoiter of their backtrail, uncertain of what he expected.

He always thought better in the saddle, giving Shady his head and letting Lobo scout ahead, he began to ruminate about the pending attack and how best to meet the renegades. As he thought, he remembered his father saying, "You can't deal with the wicked on the same terms of an honest man. The wicked have only one thing in mind, that's to take advantage of you, and they will do it any way they can. To overcome them, you have to think like they do, set aside your fair-mindedness, and replace that with the absolute will to survive, realizing that your life hangs in the balance. Then and only then will you be able to meet them and beat them." As Tate thought about it, he began to think about what he would do if he was the attacker of a wagon train full of farmers. Then he added in the thoughts of a man full of vengeance, renegade Indians that had no regard for life and a determination to take everything. As he began turning it all over in his mind, each thought seemed to increase his own anger and determination.

CHAPTER ELEVEN
RENEGADES

THE LANCE STRUCK THE LOG WITH AN ECHOING THUMP, feather and scalp lock swinging. Hoots' horse shied, but he brought the animal to a stop, searching the surrounding trees. No sound or movement came, even the usual whisper of the wind in the pines and the oft-heard trilling call of the red-wing blackbird was silent. Hoots watched for movement and in his impatience, he called out, "Is this the way the great Flat Nose greets a friend?"

A moment later, the figure slowly moved from the shadow of a large spruce toward the intruder. The man stood with burly arms bearing metal bands above the biceps crossed over a hair pipe and bead breastplate that covered a broad chest. Loose hair, tufted with bits of fur and three notched feathers, hung over well-muscled shoulders. Fringed leggings framed a breechcloth and topped beaded moccasins. As Hoots looked at the man, two others, similarly attired, stepped forward, one with an arrow nocked in a bow, the other holding a lance, ready to be thrown.

The central figure, Flat Nose, judged by Hoots as the leader of the group, asked, "Why does Owl that Walks come?"

"To share your fire and to talk of plans," answered Owl, it was not the way of the natives to immediately speak of the reason for visits or plans, that was considered to be impolite or rude. It was the common practice to share a meal or a time of talking before approaching the topic of the visit. Once pleasantries were passed, then if agreeable, the more serious subject would be considered. At Owl's remark, Flat Nose dropped his arms from his chest, and with a slight nod of his head, bid Owl to follow.

As they entered the camp, Owl noted the lack of lodges, only some brush huts and lean-tos testified of the temporary nature of this camp. Beside the three men that were with him, he saw four other men, three women and no children. Owl followed Flat Nose to a fire before one of the brush huts, a woman was busy tending a hunk of meat suspended over the fire with a metal rod spit, a pot sat near the fire on a flat rock, and the woman was adding something to her cooking. After seating himself on a robe spread near the fire, Flat Nose motioned for Owl to join him. They were no sooner seated, when the woman sliced off generous portions of the meat, placed them on a wood platter and held them before the men. Each man took one, bit into it and sliced off the rest with a quick slash of their knives.

In a short while the men were finished, and Flat Nose leaned back on his willow backrest and looked at Owl and said, "It has been a long time when we were together."

"Yes, two summers. You were still with the people."

Flat Nose nodded his head as he looked at Owl, "Our chief, Big Medicine, sent me away. He was wrong, but our enemy, the shaman Big Bear Running, spoke against me, like he did you. He is afraid of any warrior that is stronger."

Both men sat silent for a while when finally Owl began, "I come to tell you of a raid that could be big medicine."

Flat Nose leaned forward, anxious to hear, and said, "Tell me of this medicine."

"There are many wagons, this many," and he held up two hands, pulled down one finger, to indicate the number nine, "they have rifles, powder, women, blankets, and more."

"How many fighters?"

"This many," answered Owl, holding up two open hands, "but not proven fighters. There are that many women and more."

"Where do they go?" inquired the leader.

"To cross the mountains of the Wind River. They are what the white men call farmers, men that do not fight, but dig up the soil and plant corn and other things," explained Owl. Many of the native people would plant corn and squash and other plants whenever they made their summer camps. The Comanche and Cheyenne were both known for planting small crops to provide winter stores.

"How do you know of this?" asked Flat Nose.

"I rode with some white men who were trappers before, but they were scouts for the wagons. They want me to get our people to join them to take the wagons." He looked around the camp and added, "We do not need the white man. With your warriors, we could do this. If we can get more, that would be good," suggested Owl.

"Where are the wagons now?" asked Flat Nose.

"They follow the trail beside the river the white man calls North Platte. We could be at the wagons in two hands of days," answered Owl.

Flat Nose looked at his friend, considering what he had said, searching his eyes for any sign of deception and seeing none, said, "I will talk to my people."

Although most bands of native peoples have a traditional hierarchy, the leaders are not absolute rulers. Although some are chiefs or leaders of the village or band, and others are sub-chiefs, like war chiefs and others, they only lead at the discretion of the people. At any time, any warrior can mount a raiding party or hunting party, as long as he can get others to join him. If he is a respected leader, many will follow, seeking honors gained in such a raid. But if that man fails and the raid or hunt is not successful, few will follow him again. The only time any warriors are obligated to join in the fight is if the people are at war with another tribe or people and they are fighting for the entire village or tribe. The safety and security of the village is paramount.

When Flat Nose gathered the men of his small village, he knew they were not obligated to join him, but he also knew his people were struggling to survive. This had not been a bountiful summer; game had grown scarce with the minimal rains in the Spring, and none had rifles to aid in their hunting. He thought his people could use some sort of victory to build them up, but if he failed in his leading, they would leave him. As they gathered near, Flat Nose stood and began, "Our friend, Owl that Walks, has told of wagons of the white men that have much that would help us. These wagons have rifles, blankets, horses, and more. We could take them, and with the rifles, our medicine would be great. These wagons," he held up his two hands, fingers extended, "this many, are moving near the North Platte River. Each wagon has one man, one woman."

It is usually the nature of a fighting man, especially young and unproven ones, that they have an abundance of confidence, thinking themselves to be better fighters than their enemies. When they are outnumbered by the enemy, their disdain for the fighting ability of their enemy causes the warrior to consider himself to be the match of the greater number of opponents. Unless those numbers are overwhelming. When these warriors were told there were only ten enemy white men, they believed their seven warriors to be greater than the larger number of white men.

One of the young warriors known as Crooked Arrow, stood and said, "This is good to hear. We have waited here, hiding, and our bellies are getting hungry. To go after these wagons and get rifles is good. We should go." He looked around at the others, several nodding their heads in agreement, and he sat down with a smug smile.

An older warrior, called Buffalo Horns, spoke without standing, "You said these white men have rifles and we have none. They are more, it will be hard to take them."

Flat Nose replied, "Owl that Walks said we could get others to join us. We know of those led by the Sioux, Crazy Elk, there are this many," he held out one hand, "that ride with him. I believe they would come with us."

Several of those seated around the fire nodded their heads, grunting to one another, commenting as they agreed with their leader.

Stands on Black Rock, who filled the role of their shaman, although not a true shaman, stood to speak and said, "Our leader, Flat Nose, believes this to be a good thing. We are in need, but the travel could be hard for our village. I say we should take these wagons."

He sat down without looking at the others, but their mumbling remarks were in agreement and prompted Flat Nose to speak again, "Then we will go. At first light."

As the others stood to leave, the chatter among them and their expressions showed their excitement. For several days, they had grown sullen and even angry, but now with a purpose, even the women began to move with a lighter step, and laughter was heard among the people. Flat Nose looked at Owl and said, "It is good. You have done well, my friend."

Owl looked at Flat Nose as the two clasped forearms and Owl began to think of Bear and the other white men. A grin began to tug at the corner of his mouth as he thought of what the big white man that smelled and what he would think when the renegades took the wagons before him.

CHAPTER TWELVE
BACKTRAIL

THESE WERE THE MOMENTS TATE SAVORED. ALONE, ON horseback and with Lobo alongside, the vastness of the prairie with the granite peaks in the distance still holding to some patches of snow, and the whisper of the wind that carried the sounds of the wilderness. This is what he and his father had dreamed of and talked about when they were together in the woods of Missouri, hunting for meat. Sometimes the two would stand by the rail fence in the backyard and his Pa would point out the various constellations and Tate remembered asking, "Are they the same out west in the mountains?"

"Mostly, but some of the constellations would be in a slightly different orientation or position in the heavens when you're farther west. Now, if you were somewhere below the equator, the heavens would be totally different," explained his teacher father.

Tate remembered his father telling him about the differences and the use of the stars for navigation on the high seas, many things he marveled at, but soon forgot. He thought how that was the way of learning, many things seemed to catch a person's attention, but would be dismissed or forgotten with the lack of use, but the many lessons learned in the mountains, he locked away in his mind and heart.

As the grulla ambled along the path, Tate scanned the surrounding terrain, taking note of the lessons learned as he identified the vegetation, sage, buffalo grass, gramma, prickly pear, piñon, juniper, and cholla. He saw the bushy tail of a scampering red fox chasing a big-footed and long-eared jackrabbit, heard the cree cree call of a circling hawk, felt the shadow of a golden eagle as it swooped down with its extended talons to capture a fat prairie dog. Tate thought that these were the lessons that would not be forgotten or filed away with distant memories. And these were lessons he could teach his father, if he had one more day to walk the land with his Pa.

Suddenly, the grulla pulled up, head high and ears forward, looking beyond the talus slope that fell from the rim-rocked mesa. Desert bighorns, rarely seen, were mounting the rocks, seeming to bounce from stone to stone where there was little footing, yet they were not alarmed. The little ones were prodded on by the ewes, while a big full-curl ram stood watch. The cream-colored rumps were the only giveaway as their coats blended perfectly with the dusty rock formations. Within moments, the only evidence of their passing was the falling of a few small dislodged stones that tumbled to the shoulder below.

The grulla relaxed, looking around and waiting for some cue from his rider. Tate gave a slight knee pressure and the gelding stepped out. The trail was a little used game trail that paralleled the river but kept to the edge of the bluffs. With the main trail or roadway between them and the river, Tate had the advantage of easily found cover among the rocks and scattered juniper that found footing in the clay soil of the hillsides.

Tate shaded his eyes as he looked at the position of the sun, calculating the time. Guessing it to be mid-morning, he searched the rimrock of the nearest mesa for some sign of a break or notch that would provide access to the flat-top. Tate gave the grulla his head as he continued searching the rimrock for some trail. A short-while later, a fall of rocks betrayed the presence of a trail and Tate reined Shady back into the ravine to find the beginning of the trail. He was surprised to hear the chuckling of water as he rode into the ravine, rounding a slight bend he saw a cluster of willows and chokecherry, framed by a few stunted cottonwoods. Grass covered the shoulders of the bank of a small pool, fed by a spring that seeped from a sheer wall of redstone. Tate looked to the bottom of the ravine, saw only moist dirt that faded into a totally dry and sandy creek-bottom. It was an unusual little oasis, water springing from rock and disappearing into the sandy creek bottom no more than twenty yards down the ravine. He reined the grulla to the small pool and stepped down for a deep refreshing drink of the cold snow melt water. He sat back on his haunches and looked around the oasis, noting where snowmelt and rainfall came from atop the mesa and made a waterfall that smoothed the cliff face, and away from the pool, there was an overhang of rock that would be a good shelter. He could trace the path of the flash flood waters as they forced their way to the river beyond. This was one of those places that men of the wilderness would tattoo on their memories in case they needed a hidden getaway.

He swung aboard the grulla and pointed him up the trail to the mesa top. Once atop the flat, he searched the rim for a good point, and seeing one he tied off the grulla to a scrub cedar for a little shade, took his spyglass from the saddlebags and walked to the edge, dropping into a crouch as he neared his chosen outlook. He bellied down as he moved to the top of the rimrock, Lobo crawling beside him in an imitation of his master. Tate scratched the big wolf behind his ears and whispered to his friend, "We need to see if we can find them varmints, Lobo. If you see 'em 'fore I do, tell me 'bout it. O.K.?" He was certain the wolf understood as he began to look below the crest of the mesa. Tate followed suit and put the spyglass to his eye to begin his search.

Anyone experienced at hunting knows that the first thing to watch for is movement. A perfectly camouflaged or hidden animal can remain unseen until it moves. Tate searched the wide panorama of rolling hills and flat top mesas and the many game trails between for any indication of movement or life. He spotted a small herd of antelope with their bold tan and white markings and stark black horns lazily grazing in the flats, three deer, one with antlers sprouting, were making short work of some grass near the river. Three coyotes, two fox, several jackrabbits, and two more deer later, Tate looked over to Lobo and said, "I ain't seen nothin' of them renegades, have you?"

With no response from his companion, Tate decided on one more scan. He slowly moved the scope across the plains, cautiously examining every trail, ravine, gully and rock formation for any sign. Suddenly a small cloud of dust showed beyond a finger ridge that fell from the far bluff and he put his scope on it to see the cause. He watched as the wispy cloud moved, thinking it was the right size for a group of five riders. But as the cloud moved beyond the finger ridge, he saw it was nothing more than a dust devil, or a whirlwind of dust and tumbleweeds caused by the shifting winds of the prairie. Tate realized he had been holding his breath and let it out, sucking in the fresh air of the flat-top, as he crabbed his way back from the edge. Lobo walked beside, repeatedly looking up at Tate, as if waiting for a command or reward.

The three companions, Tate, Shady, and Lobo, had turned back to the west and were following in the tracks of the wagons. Tate calculated, based on his backtrail search, that any followers or pursuers were at least three days, perhaps more, behind them. He knew that men bent on attacking the wagons would make better time than the train, but time and distance were servants of no man. While the renegades were intent on their pursuit, the wagons were equally intent on their escape. As Tate traveled, he began calculating the possibilities of defense and survival of any attack by a larger and deadlier force. As one idea would surface, he would turn it over and around in his mind, examining all possibilities, then go to the next idea. He also knew the people of the wagons were considering other means and plans for their defense.

Dusk was dropping the curtain on the remaining daylight when Tate rode in among the wagons. He was warmly greeted, and two different families invited him to share their meal. He stopped at the wagon of Henry Hyde and asked, "Have you fellas come up with anything special in the way of fightin' off them scalawags?"

"Well, we haven't talked about it yet, ain't had the chance, but we figger to get together after we eat. You'll join us, won't you?" asked Henry.

"Plan on it. I'm thinkin' we got a few days, but we'll talk about it later." Tate nodded his head as he turned away and moved back to the wagon of the Heatons' to join the family for their meal.

Hettie was tickled that Tate had joined them. She knew he had taken a meal with several others, but this was the first time she had worked up the courage to invite this mysterious man to join them for a meal. She nervously puttered about preparing everything, wanting to impress the young man that she had begun to view almost as a savior of the wagon train. After their difficult experience with Bear and his partner, the relief shown by the entire company of farmers and their families had turned this arduous journey into one of purpose and even somewhat of a pleasure. They had begun focusing on their dreams again, rather than the difficulties of the journey, and for that she was thankful.

Before they left Saint Joseph, Hettie had occasionally substituted for the teacher of their small school at the edge of town. With twenty-one students and every level from beginners in the first grade to older students in the upper grades, it had been a challenge but one she enjoyed. She hoped they would soon build a school in their new home, wherever that might be, even though there were few school age children traveling with them. But she knew, several of the younger couples were planning on having large families, once they settled down in the new territory, and new and growing families with plenty of children. When their dinner-table conversation revealed that Tate's father had been a teacher, Hettie Heaton took over the conversation as she began to talk about the joys of teaching and the many students she remembered.

Tate politely listened and as she spoke, remembering the poor treatment his father had received from the village leaders where he last taught, and the way they practically ran Tate out of town after his father was killed. They were more concerned about the next teacher and the cabin Tate and his father occupied, than they were about the welfare of a young man, suddenly alone in the world. His shoulders lifted as he sighed, then his thoughts were interrupted by Hettie saying, "I'm sorry, I've just gone on and on and it must be hard on you, remembering your father."

"Oh, it's not that m'am. Thoughts of my father and my mum are special treasures to me. I often spend time alone with those thoughts, remembering all the good times together."

"Oh, that's wonderful. What a fine man you are, Tate Saint. I'm certain if your parents could see you now, they would be very proud," replied Hettie.

"Thank you m'am," answered Tate, "but I must ask for you to excuse me. The men are getting together to discuss our plans and I need to be there."

"Oh, of course, of course. And thank you for joining us, Tate."

"Thank you m'am, it was an excellent meal. Thank you for inviting me."

He turned away and Lobo, roused from his slumber at Tate's side, trotted after his friend. Several of the men were already gathered on the river's side of the Hyde's wagon, and a couple were lighting their pipes as they waited for the others. Weston Hillyard was absentmindedly whittling on a stick, to no purpose than to make a little stick out of a big one, occupying his hands in the process. His son, Mark, one of the substitute scouts, stood by his side. As Tate neared the group, the ever-nervous Russell Prescott began to rapid-fire questions at him, causing Tate to say, "Hold on, hold on, let's wait till everybody gets here. Then we'll all talk about what we're facing and how to deal with it."

The cowed Prescott stepped back and put a foot up on the wagon tongue, trying unsuccessfully to appear nonchalant. It was just a little while before the rest of the men had joined the group and Henry Hyde, ever the leader and moderator of any get-together, began with "Fellas, you heard Tate when he told us about Bear an' his pack o' varmints that're followin' us, and we've all had a day to give it some thought, so, now's the time we can put our heads together an' figger out what we're gonna do. So, before we start sproutin' ideas, how 'bout we hear from Tate first?" There were mumbles of agreement and Henry motioned for Tate to speak.

Tate stood before the men and started with, "Now, fellas, I ain't no expert 'bout much of anything, but here's what I know. When I scouted our backtrail, there was no sign of anybody within what I'd reckon to be two or three days. Now, that don't mean there ain't nobody followin' us, it just means, if there is, they are at least three days behind. I plan to keep an eye on our back trail so we'll know as soon as anybody is any nearer. But there's somethin' you need to know," he picked up a stick and squatted down to start drawing in the dirt, "Now here's the North Platte, it bends back south about a day or two ahead, and our trail follows the river. But, about a day south of that big bend, we come on the Sweetwater, 'bout here," he said, pointing in the dirt. "Now, less'n a day's travel after we hit the Sweetwater, we come onto a big ol' rock, called Independence Rock, then there's Devil's Gate and the trail stretches out toward South Pass. Now, here's what you need to know," he pointed with the stick to the mark indicating the North Platte, "we gotta follow the river, but if they know the country, they might cut across here." He drew another line straight across from the North Platte to the confluence with the Sweetwater, "And they'd cut off about a day or so of their travel, catchin' up to us sooner, an' I wouldn't see 'em on the backtrail."

"So, based on what you're saying there, let's see, that would mean they still wouldn't catch up to us for at least a couple of days, maybe longer, if they took the cutoff. But with us still travelin', that'd mean it might not be for maybe four or five days 'fore they'd actually catch up to us an' by then, we'd be somewheres around that Independence Rock. That what you're sayin'?" asked Lucas Colgan, in his somewhat gravelly voice.

"That's about it," answered Tate. "So, what ideas did you fellas come up with?"

Matthew Webster spoke up and said, "I think we need to arm the womenfolk."

Several nodded their heads and Tate answered, "Do you have enough rifles to do that?"

"Well, most of us have at least one rifle, some have more, and some have shotguns and handguns," replied the eager Webster, glad the men had listened to his suggestion.

"Well, that's good. Now you men know your women, so, if they know how to shoot, well and good. If not, you need to teach them to load for you, and maybe as you get a chance, show 'em a thing or two 'bout shootin'." Tate looked around and saw Jeffrey Pickett step forward, "I think we need a plan 'bout how to arrange the wagons and animals and be able to do it right quick."

The men continued to share ideas and discuss their options well into the night, and as they dispersed to their wagons, most were feeling more optimistic about their future, even with the threat of attack. They knew before they left Saint Joseph that this would be a trip with many challenges, including the very real possibility of Indian attack, and now they were confident they could overcome even this latest challenge to their dreams.

CHAPTER THIRTEEN
DESPERADOES

GRAMPS HAD BEEN SENT TO THE TAVERN, IF SUCH IT COULD BE called, in the building beside the trader's store of Fort William. He had been told to recruit some men for their attack and ransacking of the wagons. Before Gramps' love of liquor and ladies became his downfall, he had been a promising professor at the Lebanon Seminary in Lebanon, Illinois. But the strict standards of the seminary were too much for this young man who prided himself in his appearance and appeal to the ladies. His prematurely gray hair gave him a distinguished appearance that ladies found alluring and trustful. But when the element of liquor was added, Quentin Lawdsbury was a man without scruples or trust. Run out of town on a rail, the would-be Don Juan found himself homeless and penniless and turned to gambling and robbery to make his way. When a big beast of a man called Bear took the budding thief and immoral Quentin under his wing, he soon became the 'front' man of a duo of desperadoes. Now, he had begun to think he was no more than an errand boy for a merciless and unrelenting monster called Bear. But Gramps' fear of the man kept him from leaving and prompted his willingness to yield to Bear's demands.

Standing at the plank counter in the tavern, Gramps looked around the room, seeing two tables with men. One had men in canvas britches and galluses with homespun shirts, looking like they were workers at the Fort. The other table had two men, staring at their drinks and soaking up the sunlight streaming in through the four-paned window. The larger of the two, full bearded, broad shouldered and clad in dirty buckskins, growled at the other man, "Like I said, what're we gonna do now? Ain't got no traps, no money, cain't pay the livery for our horses . . ." he let the remark fade as he looked back at the almost empty cup before him.

The second man, also with dirty buckskins, dirty hair that barely parted enough to reveal a scarred and whiskered face, answered, "How'm I s'posed to know? I ain't got no ideas, but I durn shore got a empty belly!"

Gramps sidled over to the two men, asked, "Got room for another'n?"

The two men looked up at Gramps, at one another, and the larger man waved a hand and answered, "He'p yo'self." Gramps noticed the way the man looked at him. With his fastidious ways, Gramps was a far cry from what these two men represented, and he knew they were thinking of him as an answer to their peril. But their idea, probably to take whatever money Gramps had, by hook or by crook, was not one that appealed to Gramps. As he sat down, he motioned to the bartender to bring the men another drink, which brought a smile to the men as they lifted their heads and introduced themselves. The larger man said, "Wal, that's mighty friendly of you. My name's Sullivan, most just calls me Sully, an'," nodding his head toward his companion, "this hyar's Patrick Flynn, but we call 'im, Moose, cuz when he's sleepin' he sounds jus' like a bull moose!" The big man laughed and slapped Moose on the back as he looked to see the bartender bringing a bottle to refill their cups.

After the barkeep left, Gramps leaned into the table, lowered his voice and asked, "I heard you men talking and I might have an answer for your dilemma."

"Our what?" asked Sully.

"Your dilemma, you know, since you men are without funds and prospects, my friends and I might be of help to you," explained Gramps.

"Wal, I ain't sure what you said, but I understood funds and help an' I'm interested," declared Moose, and Sully was nodding his head in agreement.

"Well, if you're not too, shall we say picky, about what you're willing to do, then if you're willing to join us, we'll get your horses from the livery and some supplies and be on our way."

Sully looked at Moose, they nodded their heads to one another, and with one up of their cups they drained the liquor and they stood to follow Gramps from the room. Once they were outside, Sully stepped beside Gramps as they walked to the livery and asked, "Just what is it you be wantin' us to do?"

Gramps looked at the man and replied, "Does it matter?"

The big man chuckled and said, "I s'pose not!"

Gramps was pleased to find the men had two packhorses in addition to their regular mounts. He paid the bill at the livery and the men walked their horses as they strode with Gramps to the camp in the trees by the river. Bear struggled to his feet as they neared and when Gramps introduced the men to Bear, he grunted his satisfaction as he shook hands with the newcomers and offered them coffee from the pot at the fire. He spoke to Gramps as he said, "Now, if Gimpy'd hurry on back, mebbe he'll have a couple renegades to come with, and we can get outta hyar."

As they waited for Gimpy's return, the two new additions questioned Bear about the job. He growled his responses as he began to tell about the wagons, the women, and the money. When he told about the younker that had taken his job, his vehemence made him spit his remarksas he told of his eagerness for vengeance.

Gramps chimed in with, "And to top it all off, that younker, as he called him, took Bear down with a quick fist and a hard kick! That's why he's limpin' around."

Bear barked at Gramps, "He was lucky, tha's all. The sneaky punk kicked me."

Gramps knew better than to push Bear any further and turned his attention to his coffee. Sully looked up and asked, "Is that yore other man?" motioning with a nod of his head toward a small group coming their direction.

Bear looked up and seeing Gimpy leading, he answered, "Yup! 'Bout time too!"

Gimpy hobbled up with his usual hopping gait and his built-up boot on his club foot. Three Indians followed, each leading a horse bearing blankets and parfleche. Gimpy stood before Bear and motioned to the men and said, "I promised these men plenty of whiskey and a rifle each if they'd come with us to take them wagons."

"Good, wit' these and what Hoots gets, it'll be 'nuff. Git 'ny horses?" asked Bear.

"Couldn't get horses, none o' them injuns'd give 'em up," answered Gimpy.

Bear looked at Sully and said, "We'll use your'n."

Gimpy said, "Don'tcha wanna know who they is?" motioning toward the Indians.

"Alright, tell me!" grumbled the big man.

He motioned the three warriors forward, and started, "This 'uns Coyote Running, that there's Wolf sumpin' or other, and the other'ns Turtle Shell."

Bear grunted in response, looking the three over. Coyote was the biggest of the three, but still stood a handbreadth less than Bear. He had broad shoulders, braids with two feathers, and a fringed shirt and leggings, both bearing scalp locks. His eyes flashed anger and contempt as he turned away from Bear. Wolf was lean and proudly bore scars across one cheek and he stood bare chested showing a long and jagged scar that led from one shoulder across his chest to a lower rib. His eyes were blank, and he kept one hand on the hilt of his knife at his waist. The last man, Turtle Shell, had the shape of a turtle with a paunch that hung over the top of his breech-cloth and protruded from under his buckskin shirt. He smiled broadly and laughed, giving Bear the impression he wasn't quite right. But Bear didn't care about them, he knew they probably wouldn't live through the attack on the wagons, and if they did, he would probably get rid of them soon after.

"Alright, let's load up an' git outta here. We got time ta' make up!" ordered Bear. Everyone gathered their gear while the Indians watched and were soon packed and ready. The group of desperadoes and renegades were on their way. Bear led off as they took to the trail to follow the wagons into the wilderness and what Bear planned as his vengeance. His mind was focused on the women and the man that took his prize and he pictured himself wreaking havoc on the man and having his way with the women. His shoulders shook as he chuckled at the image and he kicked his horse to a trot as they left the fort.

————

Hoots, or Owl That Walks, rode beside Flat Nose as the group of renegades and their women left the camp behind. From their camp in the Laramie mountains, they would travel northwest to the North Platte River and the trail taken by the wagons. Owl knew they could bear to the west at any time and intersect the trail near the confluence of the Sweet-water and the North Platte, but they wanted to be certain of the location and progress of the wagons before they committed themselves to the cutoff. This would be a trip of several days, perhaps as many as ten days, and their scouts would range far in advance to give them guidance as to their route and pace. If necessary, they would leave the women in a camp and move forward without them.

The mood of the men was better than Flat Nose had seen for some time. He had sent two men to try to locate the band of renegades led by the Sioux, Crazy Elk, to try to enlist him and his men to join them in taking the wagons. Flat Nose and Owl had agreed that if they had the Sioux join them, they would take both the wagons and the white men that followed. With both groups taken, there would be many rifles, enough for all the warriors and more as a prize to recruit more renegades to join them. But if the Sioux would not join, they would use the white men to take the wagons, then they would turnabout and strike the white men at the first opportunity.

Once again, Owl pictured the surprise on the face of the one called Bear when Owl buried his lance in the hated big man's chest. Or if they did as his people were known to do, tie a naked Bear spread-eagled between two trees, and use him for practice with their knives and arrows, before burning him to test his courage. Owl's sneer betrayed his thoughts to Flat Nose and he was asked, "Do you see the one called Bear as he burns?"

"Aiiieee, he will die at my hand, or at the fire," snarled Owl That Walks.

WHEN THE DEFENSIVE PLAN HAD BEEN AGREED UPON, TATE suggested they change their traveling habits with a new wrinkle. "We need to put as much distance between us and them renegades as we can, and I think the way we can best do that is to travel at night," he suggested, but his remark brought forth many questions.

Henry Hyde asked, "How will we travel at night? We don't hardly know where the trail is in the daytime."

"If you've noticed, the moon is waxing full and the light we'll have will be more than adequate. With the boys scoutin' ahead, you should do fine," answered Tate.

"But the animals, they can't pull all day and all night. It'll kill 'em!" declared Lucas.

"That's just it, the heat of the day is harder on 'em. If we travel in the mornin' with an early start, we should get in a good six or more hours before the heat of the day. During the afternoon, we'll let 'em graze by the river and rest up, then after sundown, we can travel another six or more hours, giving us more time and more miles, without overly tiring the animals," explained Tate. He continued, "When I travel alone, I do most of it at night. It's quieter, cooler, and less risky."

"Risky? You mean like with Indians?" asked Weston Hillyard.

"Among others. Look folks, it's just a suggestion. You are the ones that have to do the work, so, you talk it over and decide. Whatever you do, I'll still be scoutin' our backtrail," said Tate.

Each evening, after their meal, couples worked together on their weapons. Some of the women were taught how to load the rifles and pistols, and those few experienced shooters among them, taught the others marksmanship. Although Tate had encouraged them to limit any shooting after dark, he allowed enough time for some practice before the wagons pulled out for the day. He was pleased to find out that there were ample rifles or shotguns for everyone. Although some of the women would be using smooth bore shotguns, each had become quite capable of wielding a deadly weapon. There were few pistols among the farmers and those were all single-shot cap and ball with the exception of Felix Robidoux who had a double barrel pistol. But with all the men and women armed, Tate believed they could mount a surprising defense with continuous volleys of fire-power. He also had them practice their harnessing and hitching of the mules, with a greater emphasis on unhitching so the animals would be quickly sheltered in the midst of the circle of wagons and their defensive positions readily manned. Every noon break and each evening, they practiced circling and unhitching the wagons and were becoming quite adept.

For three days and nights, the travel was uneventful and the terrain unchanging, but on the fourth day, they came to the big bend of the North Platte and the trail turned south. For the previous two weeks, even before reaching Fort

William, the terrain was almost monotonous with rolling hills, scattered juniper, an abundance of all varieties of cactus and rim-rock mesas. As the trail turned to the south, the land seemed to become even more desolate. Wide stretches of alkali covered flats were bordered by rocky ridges cut by ravines as if some great clawed creature scratched at the surface of the earth. That morning when the trail moved away from the river to mount a long razor-back ridge, a wide ravine cut basin of orange colored soil and stone spread fan-like back toward the river bottom. It was an unusual formation and the dirt-conscious farmers were amazed at the changing soils and terrains in this forsaken country. They were even more amazed when less than two miles further, the soil on both sides of the trail became a dusty purple, the likes of which none of the farmers had seen. And when the trail began to descend into a wide basin, off to the east a long arching ridge and the many smaller ridge-like fingers held a thick layer of alkali that gave the appearance of deep snow in the summer.

As the travelers marveled at the unusual terrain, Gertrude Pickett pointed out an uncommon rock formation to her husband and his inattention caused one of the front wagon wheels to crash into a large rock at the edge of the trail, busting the metal tire, splitting the rim and shattering several of the spokes, bringing the wagon to a sudden halt. Gertrude was jolted in her seat, prompting her to immediately begin berating and haranguing her husband for his carelessness. Jeffrey had jumped down from the seat and was standing, one hand on his hip, and the other removing his hat as he looked at the wheel, shaking his head.

Gertrude's ranting was considerably louder than usual, prompting the other wagons to stagger to a stop to check on their travel companions. The Pickett wagon was next to last in the line, followed only by Lucas Colgan, who had stopped and was walking toward the disabled wagon. When he came to the side of Jeffrey, Lucas began to examine the damaged wheel, then dropped to his knees and looked past the wheel to the axle. He stood and looked at Jeffrey as he said, "It's worse than just a wheel, your axle's split too."

By this time, Gertrude had joined the others that had congregated to survey the damage and when she heard the remark of the big blacksmith, she started in on her husband, "If you had been paying attention to your driving, this wouldn't have happened. Now you've got us in a fix. Just how do you propose to get us out of this mess now, mister smarty pants?" She stood, slightly bent at the waist, shaking her finger at her husband with every syllable of her tirade.

Jeffrey usually was silent and stood with a hangdog expression during his wife's many lectures. But now he looked at her with a sternness, stepped right in front of her and looked her in the eye and quietly said, "That's enough."

The woman was startled and froze in her stance with her finger still pointed up in the air and her mouth open. She tried to scowl her husband into submission, but he stood firm and she stopped all movement. Slowly dropping her head and gaze, she folded her hands in front of her, and quietly said, "Yes, dear."

Jeffrey turned away from his wife and looked to Lucas and said, "What should I do?"

Lucas let a grin paint his face and said, "Well, you've already done the hardest part. But for now, help me get my tools and the spare axle outta my wagon, and your woman can drive mine on and you and me'll stay an' fix yours."

Henry Hyde spoke up, "You don't mean you'll stay behind, do ya'?"

"You'll be stoppin' for the noonin' an' won't be movin' on till after sundown. If'n we work at it, we should get 'er fixed and catch up wit' ya' 'fore night," explained Lucas. Without waiting, he motioned for Jeffrey to follow him to his wagon. Fortunately, the ground to the opposite side of the trail was flat and unobstructed where Lucas pulled his wagon around the Pickett wagon. The men offloaded the spare wheel from the Pickett wagon, and from Lucas' wagon the axle and his tools. With Jeffrey holding both Lucas' and his own rifles, the two men waved the other wagons on, with Gertrude at the reins of Lucas' wagon. The others traveled no more than three miles before they came to the feeder creek that would lead them to the Sweetwater River, but they chose to take their nooning beside the smaller creek.

Lucas worked steadily, using Jeffrey mostly as a stepn-fetchit helper, but there were several times the work required four hands. After unhitching the team of four and picketing them by a patch of junipers, they started the disassembly. Within the first two hours, the tongue, hounds, bolster bands and kingpin had been removed and with the wagon box held up on stacked rocks, they were removing the axle. Lucas had stripped off his shirt and sweat was streaming down his forehead and shoulders, with the thick black hair on his chest and back glistening with the moisture. The massive man was accustomed to hard work and it pleased him to be using his brawn for a change. He lay on his back on a blanket as he struggled to free the axle and grunted with the exertion as Jeffrey watched.

SUDDENLY A SHOT BROKE the stillness and the twang of a splattering and ricocheting bullet startled them both. Jeffrey jumped, hitting his head on the edge of the wagon box then turned to see Tate sitting on his grulla, holding his pistol with a thin trail of smoke curling from the muzzle, and chuckling. He pointed to the trailside and Jeffrey looked to see a headless eight-foot-long fat diamondback rattlesnake, still squirming. "One of you should be keepin' watch." Tate was returning from his backtrail scout and he spoke from horseback. When Jeffrey spun around to see him, Lucas just grunted and continued working.

Jeffrey stood and shielded his eyes as he looked up at Tate and said, "You're right. We were just so concerned about gettin' this fixed, I plumb forgot."

Tate stepped down from his saddle and leaned to look at Lucas and asked, "You need some help under there?"

"I just 'bout got it, but you can take this axle soon's I get it free," replied Lucas.

It was well after dark as the men finished the wagon by moonlight. Lucas stood to the side and said, "I'm hopin' they're near a stream. I stink so bad, even the mules are skittish!"

"Well, there's a stream up yonder a ways, but I'm hopin' they've already started out for the night. But, I'm sure you can take a quick dip 'fore movin' on. You fellas lead out and I'll follow," instructed Tate as the two men climbed aboard the wagon. Lucas motioned for Jeffrey to take the lines and he leaned back, savoring the cooler night air. Jeffrey had cut the rattles from the snake and patted his pocket as he told Lucas, "That rattler had fourteen rattles an' a button. He sure was a big 'un. I'd hate to think what he'd do to a fella."

Lucas chuckled and said, "Ya know, of course, even a baby rattler's deadly. Don't matter how big he is, that poison'll kill ya, sure 'nuff. Tate said some Injuns'll dip their arrows in the poison so even a arrow in your arm or leg'll kill ya."

"Well, I'd just as soon not have to find out," answered Jeffrey.

As Tate hoped, the wagons had already started on their night's journey, but the stream was too inviting for the men to pass. Taking turns standing guard, the three were soon refreshed and definitely smelling a lot better after they washed bodies and clothes in the cool creek water. Before the wagons stopped for the last time of the night, the Pickett wagon with Jeffrey and Lucas, followed by Tate had caught up and joined the circle for the few hours rest before the early morning start.

CHAPTER FIFTEEN
CONFLICT

THE TWO BIG MEN, BEAR AND SULLY, HAD BUDDIED UP AND were now riding beside one another, talking about their plans for the wagons and other plunder.

"From whut ya' been sayin' 'bout them wagons 'n such, don't sound like thar's 'nuff to go 'round wit' all them whut's gonna be in the fight," mulled Sully.

Bear scowled at the man, glanced back at the others, and growled, "Don't plan on sharin'. Them Injuns ain't gonna last, won't be much hep' as it is, 'n I ain't too sure 'bout some o' them others neither."

"Uh huh, I see we been thinkin' th' same. Now, I know ya' ain't gonna be cuttin' me out, but which o' them others ya' skinnin'?"

"Do you care?" asked Bear, giving a sidelong glance to Sully.

"Not one whit!" answered Sully.

"Good, cuz a two-way split's 'bout as high as I can count," chortled the burly Bear.

After the band of would-be cut-throats came across the sign of the buffalo hunt and the remains of the Indian village,

Bear and Sully agreed to take the cross country due west short-cut and hopefully catch up with the wagons sooner, maybe even get to the Sweetwater cutoff before the wagons. When the men were discussing it, Sully said, "The way I 'member it," and he stood and pointed to the southwest, "if'n we stay at the foot o' them thar hills yonder, an' foller it west, it'll take us behind that mountain thar," pointing to a distant tree covered hump barely rising above the horizon, "an' foller a razor-back ridge into some alkali flats. After a spell, it'll take us to whar' the Sweetwater runs into the North Platte."

"That's whut I recomember too," answered Bear, who had followed the pointing and descriptions of Sully. "I'm thinkin' that'll cut off leastways a day, mebbe more."

"Umhumm, 'n from the sign o' their camp back yonder, they spent an' extry day or two hyar, 'n that'll put us e'en closer," surmised Sully, to the nodding agreement of Bear.

"Wal," he lifted his shaded eyes to the bright sun, nestling on the hilly horizon to the west, "I think we oughta go 'head 'n make camp. Get a early start in th' mornin'," concluded Bear. He motioned to the men to camp, hollered to Coyote, "How 'bout you an' Wolf thar, see if you can find us some fresh meat?" The stoic Indian glared at the big Bear and with one nod of his head, turned and motioned for Wolf to follow and the two men started toward the nearby river and the willow breaks to search for deer. Gimpy and Moose had been tasked with preparing the meal and the two men were soon busy gathering firewood and packs with the coffee pot and pans. Gimpy dug for the makings for cornbread while Moose started the fire. Gramps and Turtle took the horses to water while Bear and Sully stacked the packs and set aside the saddles and bedrolls.

The freshly taken deer provided juicy steaks for the crew, together with the cornbread and some roasted camas bulbs, it was an exceptional meal. The men were sitting around the fire enjoying the steaming hot java and full bellies when Bear noticed the big Indian, Coyote, digging around the stacks of their packs. "Whatchu lookin' fer, Injun?" hollered Bear, spitting his disgust to Coyote.

Coyote turned around with anger showing on his face, "Whiskey! Promised!" he snarled.

Bear thought to demand he leave the packs and whiskey, then with a second thought, he hollered, "It that parfleche by the tree yonder," pointing in the direction of a smaller stack of packs. The Indian looked at him, at the stack and went to the parfleche and pulled out two bottles, grinning. The other Indians grinned, and mumbling, joined their friend with the whiskey.

Gimpy looked at Bear and said, "What 'bout us? We gonna git'ny?"

"Go 'head but take 'er easy," answered Bear giving Gimpy a quick glance and a wave of his hand. Gimpy struggled to his feet and hobbled to the parfleche, grabbed a bottle and without taking a step away from the bag, he popped the cork and took a long swig of John Barleycorn. Wiping his mouth with the back of his hand, he smacked his lips and limped back to the fire to share the whiskey with his friends.

The thirsty men made short work of the one bottle and Moose was sent for a second. But when Bear saw Coyote going for their third bottle, he noticed the Indian staggering a bit. He grinned at the man and chuckled to himself and watched as Moose began passing the bottle around the campfire. Bear chugged his share but was confident of his ability to drink more than most men and saw no reason for temperance. Sully did his best to keep up with the leader of the crew, determined to show himself the better man, even if it was only to drink more than Bear.

Between drinks, Gramps asked Bear, "You think Hoots found any friends?"

"Dunno, he shoulda been here by now," grumbled Bear.

"What if he doesn't come back? We still gonna hit the wagons?" asked Gramps.

"I don't care who we got, we're takin' them wagons!" spat Bear before tipping up the bottle to take a long swig.

The men at the fire were startled when an argument broke out among the Indians, gathered near the packs. Bear stood to see Turtle and Coyote grappling over a bottle of whiskey. When Turtle fell away, still holding the bottle, Bear drew one of the pistols from his belt and snapped at shot at Turtle as he sat up to take a drink. The bullet went in just under Turtle's uplifted arm and plowed through the man's chest, exiting his back near the opposite shoulder. The big-bellied Indian slumped to the side, still clinging to the bottle. As he fell, Wolf grabbed for the bottle, not wanting to spill any of the precious whiskey. Wolf looked at his friend, lifted up the bottle to chug-a-lug as much as he could. But before he finished, Bear lifted his second pistol and shot Wolf through the throat, causing him to spit out the whiskey, mixed with blood, as his head dropped to his chest, neck broken through. He slowly sagged to the side, falling with his head on the outstretched legs of Turtle.

Coyote stood frozen, staring at Bear with the corner of his mouth lifting and his eyes narrowed to slits, daring the man to shoot him as well. With both of Bear's single-shot flintlock pistols discharged, the big man stared back at the insolent Indian and snarled, "Don't need no drunk Injuns, you can take a bottle 'n leave, or you can leave 'er be, and come wit' us after them wagons. What'chu gonna do?"

Coyote stared at the man without moving, then looked at his companions, turned away and went to his blankets. He lay down and with a glimpse toward the disgusting white man, wrapped a blanket around his shoulders and turned away from them. Bear watched until he was satisfied the man was done with his drinking, then turned to the rest of the men who sat silently, watching the vengeful Bear. They were aware of the man's volatile temper and his bent toward killing, knowing they could easily become the next target of one of his explosive tirades. None of the men were willing to provoke the already aggravated beast that stood before them. The big man looked from one man to the other and growled, "Better turn in, we're leavin' early!"

CHAPTER SIXTEEN
ALLIANCE

THE BULLHIDE SHIELD HUNG BY THE WARRIOR'S KNEE AS HE SAT on his blanket covered paint stallion. The big horse pranced in place, impatient to be in the hunt or on the chase. His spirit mirrored that of the man that sat astraddle and glaring at the man before them. This man's hair was in a tall standing roach, with long hair trailing down his back held in one strand gathered with thin strips of rawhide that also held a cluster of three eagle feathers. His torso was bare and exhibited three prominent scars, one on his right upper chest that was from a lance thrust during a battle with some Assiniboine. Another circular scar in his lower left abdomen was evidently from a bullet fired from a rifle held by a trapper, just before his throat was cut by Crazy Elk, almost decapitating him. The third scar was a wide mark that traveled from just below his neck almost to his left armpit and told the story of a knife fight over a woman he wanted but had been taken by another man. The memory of the knife-wielding man was one of a bloody corpse that lay beside the body of the woman that shunned his advances. It was that fight that caused Crazy Elk to be banished from the Sioux tribe. Because of these scars and his many battles, he had begun to think of himself as invincible and even immortal.

The man before him was Flat Nose, the leader of the group of renegades bound for the wagons. Flat Nose looked up at the stoic Crazy Elk and said, "It is good that you come. Our women are cooking a meal, come."

Crazy Elk looked at Flat Nose, remembering the times they had fought side by side, and nodding his head, slipped from the big paint stallion. He handed the lead line to one of his fellow warriors and then followed Flat Nose to the fire. The warriors that traveled with Crazy Elk slipped from their mounts and walked the horses to the edge of the clearing, picketed them, and returned to the camp where warriors of Flat Nose's band directed them to other cookfires and were made welcome.

The two leaders were no sooner seated than Crazy Elk, ignoring the custom of greetings and eating before conversation, began with, "Tell me of the wagons and goods."

Flat Nose looked up as Owl that Walks joined them and motioned to the man and said, "Owl knows of the wagons."

Crazy Elk looked at Owl expectantly and as Owl sat down, he began, "This many," holding up his hands with fingers spread, "less one. Each wagon has one man and one woman. Each wagon has one or two rifles and more supplies."

Crazy Elk looked around the camp, taking note of the number of warriors. He quickly tallied with his warriors there would be thirteen against nine white men. He grunted and asked, "Horses?"

"Wagons pulled by mules, some have horses," explained Owl. Crazy Elk lifted his head and nodded but before he said anything, Owl added, "Also other women. Young."

Elk let the first grin cross his face at this news and looked to Flat Nose's woman, anxious for the meal. He and his men had traveled for almost a week and took little time for eating except during their last stop before night. He was pleased to see Flat Nose's camp had women to cook and the thought they might soon have women of their own pleased Elk.

As the men enjoyed the meal, little was said but when finished, Elk asked, "Who are the whites and others that travel this way?"

Owl looked up at the man and asked, "White men, buckskins?"

Elk looked to Owl, held out one hand fingers spread, "This many whites, two big men, one big whiskers," motioning to his chin and chest. "Three Crow," he spat.

"They want to take the wagons. The big whiskers is called Bear. He sent me to get," and Owl motioned around, "more to help him. But Flat Nose said we do not need white men."

Crazy Elk looked at Flat Nose and said, "We fight with them or we fight them after wagons."

Flat Nose asked, "Where are the white men?"

Elk motioned to the ridge of mountains beside them and said, "There."

"Will we find wagons before them?" asked Owl.

They had already discussed the route the wagons were taking and where they anticipated catching them. The trail was well known to most Indians, having used that trail long before any white men were in these mountains. Most of the trails used by white men were nothing more than well-used game trails or migration routes of various Indian bands traveling from summer hunts to winter encampments. What some white men claimed as big discoveries were nothing more than claiming already established trails as their own. The warriors knew the route the wagons were traveling and what would be the best places to ambush the travelers.

To answer Owl's question, Elk shrugged his shoulders and said, "I do not know this."

The three men sat silent for a while, staring into the flames casting the sparks skyward and thinking. Whatever they decided, lives would be counted in the balance. If it was to be in league with the one called Bear and his men, there would be conflict over the plunder. If they took the wagons before Bear, they would probably have to fight him to keep their prize bounty. Owl knew Bear better than the others and he spoke first, "If we fight with them, he will turn on us after."

"But we can kill the whites first!" declared Crazy Elk.

"When their guns are empty, we can take them!" said Flat Nose, grinning. He believed they could turn on the former trappers before they could reload their rifles, if his own warriors knew the plan and acted together.

"Wait until the wagons are taken, then take the other white men. We move before, the battle could be lost," explained Crazy Elk.

The men fell silent again, thinking, and Flat Nose spoke, "Let us move closer to the wagons before we decide." Owl and Elk looked at the man and nodded their heads in agreement as they stood to go to their own blankets. There would be at least two more days before they found the wagons and the other white men. Then they would decide when to take the other hunters, but they knew they would take them.

CHAPTER SEVENTEEN
SWEETWATER

THEIR OBJECTIVE FOR THIS NIGHT'S MOONLIGHT TRAVEL WAS A distant mound, appearing as a dark shadow to their south. The Sweetwater river was just past that mound that marked where their trail would bear to the west and on to South Pass. For the last week and more the wagons had been pushing to try to outdistance the pursuing brigands led by the disgruntled and vengeful Bear, but this would be the place of confrontation. Everyone was tired of running and were determined to put an end to their flight.

Tate had relieved the boys from their scouting duties, knowing the possibility of his sighting their pursuers in the dark was improbable. He was resolved to finding a suitable location to mount a defense against the former trappers and any recruited renegades. It was not in his nature to run from a confrontation, but his thoughts had only been for the safety of those with the wagons. But they also had expressed their frustration with their flight and that they were resolute about dealing with Bear and company once and for all.

The gigantic granite monolith stood before him, rising from the grassy flats like some monster from below. Resembling a massive turtle with a smooth-backed shell, the moon reflected off the rounded hump, showing the loose stones and splits in the rock that marked the mound as the pattern on a turtle's back. Tate remembered the always angry snapping turtles in the Missouri woods, and their ability to break a limb with their steel trap jaws. The design on their shells was similar to the cracks and crevices of the mound, and the layered skin of their legs similar to the stacks of rocks at the sides.

He rode around the gargantuan mound, noting the shape and cuts. Nearer the river, there was a notch across the top that ended in a cutback on the south edge of the mound. When he neared the southeast edge, the Sweetwater lapped at the mound, making Tate turn back. He ground tied the grulla in the notch. The gelding stood in knee deep grass and began munching the tidbit without regard to Tate and Lobo as they started up the notch in the rock slope. Within moments, they were atop the smaller hump of the monolith overlooking the beginning of the notch and with an unhindered view of the flats to the north. Even in the dim light of the moon, he could see the white topped prairie schooners winding their way toward him. He quickly scanned the flats for any obvious signs of their pursuers but seeing none he rubbed Lobo behind his ears and turned to slip down the slope to Shady.

He rode back around to the north side of the massive rock, stepped down from his saddle and dropped his reins to ground tie the grulla. He found a smooth spot on the edge of the mound and with Lobo laying in the cool grass by Shady. Tate lay back on the rock, slipped his hat behind his head for a makeshift pillow and looked at the star-studded heavens, smiling at the many memories of star-gazing.

He was still searching the stars naming the constellations when he heard the first rattle of trace chains and squeak of wheels and scrape of rims on stone that told of the approaching wagons. Tate sat up, slapped his hat against his leg and put it on his head as he watched the wagons draw near. He recognized Russell and Rebekkah Prescott in the lead wagon and motioned them to move to the east, parallel to the mound. He stepped down and walked alongside the wagon and pointed to the notch in the mound and said, "Pull up toward those loose stones, close to the rock. I'll have the others pull in behind and make a loop out this-away," giving a swooping arc with his arm to indicate his intent.

"Will do. Does this mean we'll be stoppin' here for a while?" asked Russell.

"Mebbe so, mebbe so. We'll see what ever'body else thinks in the mornin'," answered Tate as he stepped back to motion to the next wagon.

When the rest of the wagons were in place and the men were unharnessing the mules, Tate went back to Shady and began removing his saddle and gear. Henry Hyde approached him and asked, "Think this is where we'll make our stand?"

"Mebbe. From what I can tell it looks pretty good. But, we'll all get together in the mornin' and look it over and if ever'body likes it, we'll make a plan," answered Tate as he dropped his saddle and gear at the edge of the mound. He grabbed his bedroll and saddle bags, slipped the Hawken from the scabbard and said, "Let's get us a good night's sleep and work on it in the mornin'."

"I like the sound of that. Should we post a watch?" asked Henry.

"I'm gonna be up there on top of that mound an' I can see forever in every direction. Lobo'll be with me, so, I think we can handle the watchin' for tonight. You go 'head on an' turn in. I think we'll be alright," answered Tate. Henry grinned, nodded his head and with a wave of his hand, turned away to go to his wagon and family.

A GRAY GROUND squirrel sat on his haunches with his small front feet holding a bristly cone from a piñion, searching for the thin shelled nuts, all the while staring at the sleeping Tate. Although silent in his moves, the whisper of his tail on the rock and the stare from big brown eyes made Tate's eyes pop open and stare back at the little furry rodent. Tate glanced over at Lobo, stretched out on his back with all four legs in the air and his head twisted to the side, sound asleep. He spoke softly and said, "What kind of a watch dog are you?"

Lobo seemed to squirm in four directions at once as he came awake and searched all around for what had disturbed his slumber. All he saw of the squirrel was the fuzzy end of its tail as it disappeared in a crack beneath a large boulder that seemed to be balanced on an even smaller stone. Lobo looked to Tate as if waiting for a command, but Tate just said, "Alright, alright, you're not in trouble. We weren't in any danger. I don't think the squirrel was gonna do us in for sleepin' on his rock, although he didn't look none too happy with us bein' here." Tate slapped the floppy felt hat on his head, pulled the pant legs of his buckskins down over his high-topped moccasins, and from his seated position scanned the flats. They were showing long shadows from the thin edge of the rising sun. His eyes took in the broad gray band of first light and watched as the sky and land alike was painted with the brilliant orange and pink of the rising sun.

Tate gathered his gear and started off the mound. Shady greeted him and Lobo as they stepped from the rock to the grass and Tate rubbed the grulla on his face, neck and behind his ears, much to the delight of the horse. Hank, the young son of Henry Hyde, called out to Tate and said, "Hey Mr. Saint! Ma says she wants you to come for breakfast. She's got some hot biscuits n' honey with some sliced pork belly if you're intersted'."

Tate grinned at the boy's enthusiasm and his 'intersted' remark, and answered, "Well, Hank, why don'tchu tell your Ma that I'm definitely interested and hungry too! I'll be right along." He waved the boy off and walked toward the Hyde wagon to suggest the leader of the wagons gather the men together and have a planning session as soon as everybody had their bellies full.

SOME OF THE men were still carrying their tin cups with coffee as they gathered at the Hyde wagon. Tate was waiting for them and said simply, "Follow me," as he started for the notch behind the wagons and began to climb up the mound. The men with coffee cups soon had to tie them to their belts or galluses as the climbing, although not difficult, required the occasional reaching down with their hands for balance as they worked their way to the top. Much of the monolith was too steep and slick for climbing but here at the notch, the slope was more gradual and easily mounted. When they topped out, the men stood and looked around, speechless at the panoramic view of the flats and hills and mesas that stretched as far as they could see. Those from the farmland of Missouri were accustomed to seeing no further than their neighbor's hedgerow, but now they could see for many miles in every direction. They slowly turned around looking in all directions and taking in the vistas.

Tate gave them a few moments to enjoy the sights then he began, "Now, we came from the cut in the long ridge yonder," pointing back to the north. "I think Bear and company will be coming from nearer to the river, maybe there where the orange soil turns to the white alkali. There's a trail through that notch there and that goes back to them low mountains across the river. But I been seein' some dust from that valley across the river, there," as he pointed to a narrow valley more to the south than the first trail. "When the Cheyenne told me 'bout Bear followin', he also said his scouts thought they were roundin' up some renegades to join up with 'em. So, we might be facin' more'n just Bear an' his friends."

"So, what'dya think we oughta be doin'?" asked Lucas.

"Well, I wanted you fellas to see this rock from up here and maybe get an idea 'bout what we'd best be doin'. See where the wagons are now, that's a purty good spot to defend, them rocks back by the mound would be good fall-back defenses. And with the wagons brought in a little tighter, the animals would be safer in that circle. Or," and he turned around to point behind them, "this notch back here is a bit bigger and deeper, an' narrower at the openin' with good cover on the sides."

"Yeah, but, all they'd have to do is climb these rocks like we done, an' come up behind us," observed Webster.

"Yeah, but look at them cracks and rocks. If you post a couple shooters up here on the rocks, mebbe one or two look-outs higher up, they'd be able to protect our backs and have a good field of fire out at anybody attackin'," declared Lucas. The men looked around, seeing the indicated crevices big enough to hide a shooter or a look-out and other loose boulders that would also provide cover for a shooter. They talked among themselves and motioned to different spots, considering different possibilities. Tate let them talk and listened as they discussed options. These were men that were talking about fighting for their families and their dreams. Gone were the thoughts of running away or letting the pursuers have their way, these were committed men, men that would do to ride the river with, thought Tate.

Tate was committed to letting the men lay their own plan. If he saw a problem, he was willing to point it out, but he wanted these men to make a plan they could understand and follow. He liked what he was hearing, they were talking about placement of shooters, ample ammunition, maybe even having the shooters bring a loader with them. Having lookouts on the high points to ensure none could attack from the back side of the mound and protecting the animals by using the deeper notch. He was pleased with their decision and their plan, he believed they had planned well.

CHAPTER EIGHTEEN
BACKTRAIL

MARK HILLYARD FOLLOWED TATE IN THE WANING DARKNESS of early morning. Of the two young men that had scouted for the wagons, he had been chosen as much for his horse as his marksmanship, but Tate also liked the maturity of the young man. Not talkative, but attentive, and cautious in his actions. The deliberate manner of Mark reminded Tate of himself when he first came to the mountains and was eager to learn everything about living in the wilderness when he spent time with Kit Carson. Kit had become his mentor and though little time was spent together, Tate believed he had learned more from Kit in that short while than any other period in his life. Now, he hoped to pass on some of that hard-gained knowledge to this young man. Tate had asked Mark to join him on this backtrail scout, with the intention of using him as much as a messenger as anything. Tate's primary goal was to give the wagons as much of a warning as possible before any attack came.

They left the wagons in the middle of the night because Tate wanted to be in place before daylight. Although most denizens of the wild are wary of campfires after dark, early morning fires of early risers were more common. White men especially were needful of their morning coffee and that required a fire, howbeit a small one. In the darkness, even a pinprick of light can be seen for miles, and Tate hoped to capitalize on that carelessness. On his previous scouts, Tate had spotted what he thought would be an excellent promontory that would provide unhindered views of the wide flats and rolling hills, and by his calculations they should be in place well before first light.

They were a little over ten miles east from the mound where the wagons were preparing, and north of the confluence of the Sweetwater and North Platte. His chosen spot resembled a long bony finger with the middle knuckle sticking up higher with a bald knob. The soil was orange and small clusters of juniper and piñion littered the ravines and gullies that abounded the hilly area. Those many hills bordered the deep rocky canyon that held the white waters of the North Platte. But from that promontory, Tate would have a view of the flats behind him, the trail that cut the North Platte to the north, and the other east/west trails east of his location. Without his spyglass, the brass barreled monocular he inherited from his father, this promontory would be useless, being too far from the trail. But this simple instrument gave him the advantage of seeing figures, movement, and dust many miles away. Now, he hoped it would bring him the light of distant campfires.

They tethered their horses to one of a cluster of juniper, loosened the cinches and taking his spyglass from the case, he led the way to the bald knob that would serve as their lookout post. After traveling in the darkness with the only illumination being a sliver of moon and a myriad of stars, their eyes were accustomed to the low vision and they easily made their way to the point. It was as much a ridge as a knob, but they soon found a comfortable place with a big flat-top boulder for a back rest and Tate unlimbered the spyglass and began his scan.

Using his knees for support, he started his survey on the flats behind him and to the north. With no landmarks visible in the darkness, he used his stationary body as a reference, and scanned back and forth, slowly moving the scope farther up and to the more distant plains. Seeing nothing, he started over, close in and slightly right of his first search. Each time, slowly scanning, giving his eyes time to catch any glimmer of orange or white in the darkness. Mark sat silently beside and watching, noting the thoroughness of the man before him. Lobo had found his place to the left of Tate and stretched out, chin resting on his forepaws and only his eyes searching the darkness before and below them.

As each scan proved fruitless, Tate squirmed to position himself for the next one, slightly to his right, as he worked his way around the three-quarter perimeter before them. As he completed his scan of the eastern hills beyond the canyon, he stood and stretched and watched Lobo stretch his front legs out with his rear up and move back to stretch his body its full length. Tate thought of how the wolf had grown, now standing almost waist high and probably weighing a hundred and twenty-five pounds or more, he had become a formidable beast and a worthy ally. Tate sat on the rock and handed the spyglass to Mark and said, "Here, you try it a spell. Take your time, you're lookin' for light, remember, an' it ain't gonna be very big."

Mark grinned as he took the scope and put it to his eye to begin mimicking the movements of Tate. As the young man scanned, Tate searched the vistas with his naked eye, concentrating on the creek bottomed valley directly east and the flats behind. He heard a quick intake of breath from Mark and looked to see the young man frozen, focusing the glass directly north of their location. Mark whispered, "Maybe, yeah, yeah." He turned to Tate and handed the scope to him as he said, "There, straight north, quite a ways out there, but it's a fire alright."

Tate put the glass to his eye and began searching for the fire, within moments he focused in and saw the same light. He waited, looking for any movement, maybe someone crossing before the fire, anything that would indicate men and maybe how many. But the fire was too distant, and it was only the flickering light that could be seen. Lowering the glass, Tate searched that direction for some landmark that showed in the darkness, and the dim light of early morning revealed a broad flat-top mesa just to the east of the fire. Tate knew they would be unable to discern any more until at least the gray of first light. He looked to Mark and said, "Good, ya did good. We'll wait for first light for more, but we'll keep searching for any other light until then." He handed the scope back to the young man, so he could continue the scan.

"There! There's some more!" exclaimed Mark. He was holding the scope one handed and pointing with the other to the east across the canyon. "They're closer, too!" He turned and looked expectantly to Tate who quickly took the scope to view the indicated light.

There was a cluster of three fires, close to one another, and much nearer than the previously sighted fire to the north. Tate looked closely, watching for movement, and saw shadows cross in front of the fires, and enough shadows to indicate several men. He sucked in a deep breath that lifted his shoulders and sat down to lean back against the rock for a more stable view. The magnified vision also magnified the movement and the scope had to be held steady to give a clear view. He lowered the spyglass and looked at Mark and said, "White men usually have one fire, they don't travel in large groups so one fire is usually enough. Indians often travel in larger groups and will have more fires, but smaller ones.

Since they're a larger group, they also think of themselves as the predator and aren't too afraid of anyone seeing their fires. I imagine their scouts have told 'em there ain't anybody near to be 'feared of, so they're enjoyin' their hot meal in the morning. This is their country and they see themselves as the rulers of these plains and act like it, too."

"So, you mean those fires are probably Indians?" asked Mark.

"Probably," answered Tate.

"Are they peaceable, like the Cheyenne were?"

"I don't think so. These are probably some o' them renegades or outcasts that White Hawk was talkin' about. What I don't know is if they're plannin' on joinin' up with Bear. And I think that fire to the north is Bear an' his bunch," explained Tate. "We'll keep watch on 'em 'fore we decide what we're gonna do. I wanna make sure of who they are and what their intentions might be, 'fore we go soundin' the alarm."

But they didn't have long to wait as the rising sun waits for no man. The gray band of light slowly began to change colors with the slow appearance of the fiery ball. The brilliance of the rising sun splashed across the horizon and painted the hills and flats with its colors. Because the camp with multiple fires lay directly east of their promontory, the vision of the two lookouts was hindered. Tate rose from his seat before the rock and perched himself on top, struggling to shade the front of the glass from the direct sun, so he could see those below, but also to limit any reflection that would give them away. With the bright sun directly in their eyes, they twisted and squirmed, but with Mark holding Tate's hat above and in front of the scope, Tate was finally able to get a better view.

The Indians were breaking camp and he saw a couple of advance scouts ride down into the valley bottom and closer to the canyon. The others were beginning to file away from their camp, moving in a long line of ones and twos. Still too far away for a more distinct view, Tate lowered the scope and shielded his eyes as he looked at the terrain across the canyon. He followed the creek bottomed valley from the Indian's camp toward the North Platte that ran below their promontory in the deep canyon farther below. As he looked, he saw the creek met the river well below the canyon, but above the confluence with the Sweetwater. He lifted the glass to view the joining of the creek and the river, saw what appeared as a likely crossing and assumed the band would cross there and be well north of the mound and the wagons. He looked back toward the moving band and watched their progress. He guessed their number to be near twenty, but he still couldn't tell if they were all warriors or if they had women and children with them.

He turned about to search the north for any sign of the others that had the single fire. There was no obvious sign of anyone, but he knew they would be too far distant to make out, unless they kicked up a cloud of dust. His concern was whether or not that group was Bear and company and if they were planning on joining with the renegades. But for that matter, he didn't even know if the renegades were after the wagons or just moving their camp. As he thought about it, Mark asked, "Do you think I should go warn the wagons?"

"Well, I'm thinkin' on that. What I'd like to know is if those Indians are plannin' on goin' after the wagons or not. They might just be travelin' to another camp or goin' on a hunt or sumpin' and have nothin' to do with us. But, if they are goin' after the wagons, the folks need to be warned."

Mark looked at Tate, waiting for an answer and watched as he lifted the glass again. When Tate lowered the scope, he looked at Mark and said, "Here's what'chu do. You go on back to the wagons, tell 'em what we seen. Tell 'em they need to be ready, just in case these Indians here are goin' after 'em.

And let 'em know 'bout the others too. Have 'em make sure they got somebody up on top o' that mound, so they can see when anybody gets close, maybe you could do it. I'll stay here an' see if they join up with Bear an' his bunch, that is, if that fire we saw up north was them. If I can get away to make it back to the wagons 'fore anybody else gets there, then I'll do it. But I might hafta be kinda a rear guard an' mebbe join the fight from behind 'em or sumpin'. But, if I don't make it back, you tell the folks to just foller the Sweetwater to South Pass and keep pointin' west till they find what they're lookin' for. Now, go on, and get goin' and keep your topknot on!"

IT WAS THE SAME PURPLE SOIL MARKING THE TRAIL THE
farmers traveled and marveled at where Bear and company
picked up their tracks. That morning they left their camp on
the west bank of the North Platte determined to find the trail
of the wagons so they could mount their attack. Finally, on
the trail, Bear's examination of the tracks showed they were
more than a day behind. He stood in his stirrups to check the
trail ahead and turned to tell the men they would camp when
they hit the headwaters of the creek that cut the edge of the
plain. The usual grumbles ensued, and Bear dropped back
into his saddle and gigged his mount forward.

As soon as they moved out of the wide narrow valley that
held the trail, Bear motioned the Indian, Coyote, forward
and waited for him to come alongside. He started, "Listen, I
sent one o' muh men, Hoots, to find some o' his renegade
friends to jine up wit' us an' I'ma thinkin' they be somewheres south of us." Bear stood in his stirrups and pointed to
the southeast across the flats and continued, "I want you ta'
head off down thataway, and mebbe south o' the canyon
yonder an' see if'n you can find 'em. If'n you do, tell 'em we be

comin' an' to hang out by the river till we get thar. Unnerstan'?"

Coyote looked at Bear with a slight snarl to his lip and nose as he grunted, "Ummhumm, Coyote go." He quickly jerked the head of his mount to the side and dug heels in his ribs to take off at a gallop in the direction Bear instructed. As he left, Bear snarled, "Dumb Injun, I hate 'em all!"

After sending Coyote in search of the renegades, Bear and company pushed on to the cover of the tall willows and chokecherries of the creek that bordered the west edge of the broad plateau. After the previous day's travel across the alkali and cactus flats, the cool shade and fresh water was a welcome sight for the often-angry gang of cutthroats. They made short work of laying out their camp and getting a fire started for their last meal of the day. They were beginning to run short of supplies and long on frustration making everyone's temperament somewhat volatile.

When Gimpy started his usual whining and complaining, he received a backhand from Moose that tumbled the man close to the fire. He came up with a snarl and a sharp knife flashing a reflection of the fire behind him. "I'll gut you fer that!" he barked at Moose.

The man had been seated on a big flat rock, but when he saw the flash of the knife, Moose grabbed his knife from his boot-top as he rose to a fighting stance. "I think yuh'll fin' I ain't no fish you can gut, you bag o'buffler bile you!"

The two men began to circle one another, each holding their knives blade up with their other arms stretched wide. Gimpy was surprisingly agile on his clubfoot with the built-up sole on his boot, but his eyes were searching the camp, moving from his opponent and to both sides. Gimpy's moving eyes bothered Moose, making him wonder what the man was looking for, and made him think there might be someone moving behind him. He watched the man hopping about and wondered what he was up to. Moose made a quick swipe at Gimpy's arm, missing, but it made Gimpy more watchful.

But again, Gimpy flipped his knife over with sharp edge down then looked to the side of Moose, causing Moose to turn his head to see what he was looking at and Gimpy lunged, slicing with his knife across the unprotected stomach of Moose, cutting through the loose fitting buckskin tunic, and laying bare the knife sliced and bleeding stomach.

Moose dropped his hand to his stomach, felt the cut in the buckskin, and brought his hand back, bloody. The burning sensation of the cut caused Moose to bend slightly, and as he dropped his knife hand, Gimpy swiped back-handed with his knife, laying open the right sleeve and cutting into the upper arm of Moose. This cut was deep, and blood came freely, and it limited the movement of Moose's right arm, making him switch the knife to his left hand. He knew he was in trouble and began searching the faces of the other men that stood watching the dance of the knife-fighters.

Sully looked to Bear and when the man did nothing, Sully looked back at the fighters, pulled his pistol from his belt and hollered, "That's 'nuff! Back off or I'll kill the next 'n that moves!"

Both fighters looked at Sully, saw the pistol and Gimpy rose from the fighting crouch and said, "Alright! I don't reckon he'll be backslappin' anybody anytime soon, nohow." Moose walked to the big stone and eased himself down as he slipped the knife back into its sheath at his boot.

He began looking around for something to tend to his wounds when Bear said, "Gramps, fix 'em up." Gramps rose and went to the packs to get the necessary paraphernalia to tend to the wounds of Moose. Gramps cauterized the cut on Moose's arm and put a poultice of sage leaves on his stomach cut, declared him alright and turned to do in his share of the venison and cornbread.

The following day, with no sign of Coyote, Bear decided to move farther down the creek and closer to the trail of the wagons. He sent Gimpy ahead to scout out their trail and hopefully locate the wagons explaining they would make this a short day's travel as they waited word from both scouts. No one complained until Bear sent them all in different directions to find meat for the camp.

It wasn't long before the men were drifting back into camp. Sully and Moose had gone together and came back empty handed. When Gramps pushed his way through the willows, he had a hind quarter of a deer over his shoulder and he looked at the others when he said, "I got 'nuff for me, if you fellows want some, go back yonder and get the rest of this deer."

Sully and Moose followed Bear as they back tracked Gramps to the remaining carcass of the deer and with each one carrying a quarter, the whole deer was soon lying beside the cookfire where the coffee percolated to give a welcome back. The men had no sooner skewered some steaks to hang over the fire than the sound of approaching hoofbeats made them scramble for their rifles.

When Gimpy led his horse into the clearing, he was facing the muzzles of four rifles and said, "Whoa up thar! If'n you wanna hear muh news, you'll wait till I'm done talkin' 'fore ya shoot!" The men lowered their rifles as Gimpy stripped his horse and put him with the others. He walked back to the fire, saw the steaks, counted them and went to the haunch of deer to slice himself a steak. The anxious men watched him and waited as he savored the moment of attention and control and dallied with his cut of meat. When his steak was hanging over the fire, he sat back and said, "Wal, I found 'em. They's all camped by that big ol' rock mound down thar nex' to th' Sweetwater. Saw them girls too."

"Didja see that snot-nosed kid whut's leadin' 'em?" growled Bear.

"Yup. An' it looks like they be takin' a break or sumpin'. Don't 'pear to be in no hurry, anyhow," answered Gimpy.

"Hummm, that's good. They kin jus' wait till them renegades catches up an' we'll clean 'em outta thar. Take ever' thin' they got too," growled Bear.

The rest of the men grinned at the thought their quarry had been treed and they began letting their own thoughts of plunder and pillage take over their minds. Some, like Gramps, were thinking of the money the farmers were supposed to have and what he could do with that money. Others, like Gimpy, were just thinking of the blood he could spill, and the thought of the carnage brought an evil smile to the man. But while Bear was thinking of vengeance over the young man that took his place and against the men of the wagons that cut him loose, Sully and Moose were thinking of women.

It was just before the gray of early dawn when Bear came suddenly awake and saw Coyote standing over him. He grabbed for his pistol only to find it missing. He looked at Coyote and saw a wicked grin stretch across his face as he lifted Bear's pistol before him. "I do not trust you," said Coyote. He handed the pistol butt first to the big man as he rolled from his blankets and sat up.

Bear growled, "Didja find 'em?"

Coyote nodded, "They will wait at river." He looked at Bear as if waiting for a response and receiving none, continued. "Two men crossed." He motioned toward the northeast. "Before light."

Bear lifted his eyes to the Indian and asked, "What'd they look like?"

"Young, no hair," motioning to his chin, "One buckskins," pointing to Bear's tunic.

Bear let a slow grin stretch and asked, "One in buckskins, big? Not like me, like you?"

Coyote slowly nodded his head affirmative.

"His horse, what color?" asked the whisker-faced Bear.

Coyote looked at the fire, used a stick to pull some ashes aside, and pointed to the ashes. "Horse like that."

"Good, that's the one I'm after. You swap horses with one o' them other'n, and you're comin' wit me. I need'ju ta' show me whar he went."

GIVEN THE TASK OF WARNING THE WAGONS, MARK HILLYARD left the promontory at a gallop. His well-bred Morgan gelding stretched to the task as the rising sun spread its brilliance across the broad plateau and cast the shadow of the dust that rose from the horses hooves. As Mark rushed toward the mound, Bear and Coyote watched from the edge of the ridge of the broad plateau. "One rider," observed Coyote.

Bear growled, "That means one's left on lookout, prob'ly the one I want. C'mon, let's get thar an' see if'n he's waitin' fer us."

The two men were using the contours of the land to shield their approach. Although they did not know the exact location of the lookout, they were confident they could cut his trail and follow the tracks to his position. Bear's hunger for vengeance drove him forward, as he constantly imagined what he would do to the usurper. It was only a short while until Coyote reined up as he leaned over the neck of his horse, looking at the ground. He pointed to the slightly turned up soil and said, "Here," and pointed to the east, "go there." The promontory on the narrow knob was easily seen and both men recognized this would be the best location for anyone to watch the surrounding area.

Bear and Coyote had kept themselves obscured from anyone watching by using the many contours and ravines of the area. Now at the edge of the broad plateau that was marked by the countless gullies and ravines that led to the canyon of the North Platte, they paused to consider the best route to the probable place of the lookout. Bear motioned to Coyote and spoke in a whisper, "Let's go on foot. Tie off our horses to them trees yonder. You go thataway," pointing to the right side of the finger ridge, "an I'll go thisaway," pointing to the left side. "If you get to him first, don't kill him. I wanna do that!" warned Bear. Coyote nodded his understanding and after tethering the horses, the two men started their stalk.

TATE WATCHED the dust lift behind the horse ridden by Mark. He shook his head as he thought, *I shoulda told him to take it easy. That dust cloud is just like an arrow pointin' back at me and straight ahead to the wagons.* But he knew there was nothing to be done now, just hope that Mark made it safe to the wagons. After all, there was no reason anyone would think Tate was here, besides, he was keeping watch.

With the sun up, he watched as the renegades crossed the Sweetwater and thought they were not showing any haste to their moves. He also noted there were women leading horses laden with travois and their lodges. He still wasn't sure these were renegades after the wagons or just a small band of Indians moving to some other encampment. Although there were few women and several warriors, which indicated they were a war party of sorts, there was no way to be certain. As he watched, he saw the women starting to unload the travois and apparently, they were starting to make a camp. It was early in the day to be making camp, unless this was their destination.

Tate turned to put his focus on the distant site that he thought was the location of Bear and company. Earlier there was a trace of smoke that told of a campfire, but he had seen no other activity. That camp was on the banks of the creek that fed into the Sweetwater and an abundance of willows, alders and chokecherries shielded any activity from sight. Still he watched, carefully scanning upstream and downstream, searching for any movement. Seeing none, he turned back to the camp of the Indians. As he started to lift the scope, the cold wet nose of Lobo touched his exposed wrist and he looked at his friend. The wolf stepped back, looking around and back at Tate and the man understood, "Alright, alright. You can go catch you a rabbit or somethin', I know you're hungry. Go ahead," and he motioned with his hand toward the nearby brush filled ravine.

As he watched the wolf trot off, Tate turned to once again glass the Indian encampment. His observation revealed about a dozen warriors. Typically, as the women were setting up the lodges and the men were busy with their weaponry and horses. Tate watched for a while and saw no evidence that might indicate their readying for an attack on the wagons. He was certain they knew the whereabouts of the wagons, as Indians always had scouts out and about and would have already spotted the wagons by the mound. But with nothing unusual about the camp activity, Tate thought maybe these were not the band that would be joining Bear. He sat back, putting the spyglass on the ground at the edge of the big boulder and leaned back against the rock to enjoy the warm sun.

The past several days had been trying times for Tate, constantly scouting the backtrail, working with the men of the wagons to prepare for any attack, the traveling at night, helping the young men that were scouting ahead, and the many other duties that befell the guide and scout of the wagon train. He had few opportunities to rest and now those days were beginning to catch up with him. The warm sun felt good and he could use a bit of a snooze, maybe just a short one. He never slept sound and as a light sleeper, he could still keep watch.

THE SNORT and squeal from Shady brought Tate fully awake, his head swiveling as he searched for whatever had alarmed his horse. He slowly rose to his feet, searching the trees and shoulder of the finger ridge in the direction of the tethered horse. He knew it could be anything from a coyote to a badger to a snake or a man. He slowly slipped the Paterson from the holster at his hip as he stepped slightly behind the flat-top boulder. He heard nothing, no additional warning from Shady, none of the usual sounds of the wilderness. Even the slight breeze that continually rose from the canyon below seemed to have stilled.

The flash of grey came from the other edge of the ridge and a roar of a growl caught the full attention of Tate as he saw Lobo launch himself in a flying leap toward an Indian crouched at the rocks marking the ridge. Tate could only see the head and shoulders of the man, but that was the target of Lobo as he sailed through the air, teeth bared, and struck the man with the full force of his hundred and twenty-five pounds powered with all the strength in his muscular legs. The man was frozen in shock and fear and didn't even have time to lift his arms in defense as Lobo's teeth sunk into his throat and neck and his weight bearing them both to the ground. A muffled scream came out as the Indian pushed back against the furry monster, but the scream was stifled as the massive jaws clamped down on the man's neck and the vicious shake from side to side ripped the man's throat open. The snarling and growling of the wolf held Tate's attention as Lobo continued to tear at the man's neck and shoulders.

Suddenly, Tate's hand was smacked to the side and the Paterson went flying over the shoulder of the ridge. Tate's surprise was complete and the vicious backhand from the burly Bear was accompanied with a growled, "Now I gotcha, you miserable whelp!" The backhand whipped Tate's head to the side and he tasted blood as he staggered to catch his balance. Bear followed his backhand slap with a clubbing fist from his left that knocked Tate to the ground. His face hit the dirt and he tasted blood and dust as he tried to roll to the side and get up. Before he could move, the big foot of the monstrous man kicked out and struck Tate in the side, pushing all air from his lungs and sending a wave of pain and nausea through his body. He knew that kick had broken at least one rib and maybe more. He started to draw his knees up, but Bear brought the butt of his pistol down on the back of Tate's head, knocking him into the dirt again.

Tate heard the man shout and in an instant the pistol roared and Tate thought he had been shot. But he heard the whine of Lobo and believed Bear had killed the wolf. He heard Bear mumble, "That fixed that cur of a wolf!"

Tate had drawn up his knees and was struggling to push himself up when another kick to his ribs sent him rolling to his side. Now on his back he saw the big man grinning and laughing and walking toward him. "Now, how you like it? Huh? Ain't so big now are ye? You miserable whelp you, you ain't never seen the day you're a match for Bear!" He lifted his foot to stomp Tate but was surprised when Tate rolled away and scrambled to his feet.

As Tate stood, slightly crouched, facing the big man, he reached for his tomahawk, but it was gone. Bear roared as he charged, arms wide, wanting to grab Tate and get him in a bear hug that would squeeze the life from him. But Tate, ducked under his arm and brought up a balled fist into the man's solar plexus that doubled him over. Tate stepped behind him and clasped his hands together and brought them down on the back of Bear's neck, dropping him to the ground.

Bear hit the ground but quickly rolled and scrambled to his feet, surprising the young man with his agility. Now Bear was wary and dropped to a slight stance, but moved side to side, looking for an opening to this young man that he wanted to destroy. He had always been able to use his brute strength to overpower any opponent and charged at Tate swinging wildly. Tate ducked under the roundhouse right but was surprised by the quick left that followed and hit him broadside on the jaw, sending blackness and flashes of pain into his head. Tate staggered, and Bear followed, using his big foot to sweep Tate's leg from under him. As the younger man fell, Bear brought up a knee that caught Tate full in the chest, snapping his head back and crashing him against the big boulder. He no sooner hit the ground and Bear grabbed at his collar and jerked him up, cocking his meaty right arm and balled fist to plow into Tate's face. Tate was barely able to turn his head, making the big man's fist a glancing blow, but Tate felt the pain of it.

Tate fought for footing and was pushed back by Bear, still grabbing at the young man to crush him. A left jab smashed against Tate's cheek and eye, splitting his face and smashing his nose. Bear was slobbering in his zeal and knew he had damaged the young man, but not to his full satisfaction.

Tate was bent over, holding his face and feeling the blood run through his fingers. He lifted up and could barely see the big man as he charged toward him, but Tate dropped under the swing and brought his knee up to smash into Bear's gut, once again doubling him over. But all it seemed to do was fuel the man's anger as he spun around and roared like a grizzly as he charged at the battered and bloody Tate.

Tate stood his ground and met Bear face on and for a few minutes the two mismatched fighters stood toe to toe slugging it out. Tate continued to hammer at Bear's gut and ribs, as Bear's blows landed on Tate's shoulders and side. Each blow to Tate's side increased the trauma from his busted ribs, but Tate was getting his stamina back, although badly beaten, he began to think he just might survive this, he had to, the wagons needed him. Suddenly a roundhouse with a massive fist clobbered Tate's ear and he crashed to the ground, the impact as bad as the blow. He struggled to get a breath and he couldn't see for the blackness crowding around. He tried to bring his knees up, but a sudden blow to his side with the broken ribs sent him tumbling over the shoulder of the ridge. As he rolled and slid down the steep slope, dust filled his lungs and the blackness blinded him. He felt the gravel and rocks slipping and rolling underneath him as he grasped for something to stop his slide. He realized he was slipping to the bottom of the ravine that ended at the edge of the cliff wall of the canyon of the river below. If he went over the cliff, it was a drop of almost a hundred feet to the boulder strewn river. He could not survive that fall. He was still sliding and grabbing at anything and everything. The dust cloud caused by the tumbling debris and rocks obscured his view but also hid him from those above. His hand caught an exposed root of a tenacious sage and his fall was stopped, but he could hardly breathe. He was practically buried in the gravel and rocks and unable to move as the blackness fell.

BEAR STOOD at the edge of the precipice looking down the steep ravine and seeing no movement, thought Tate had fallen over the edge into the canyon. He cackled and said, "That does it! Nobody can do in Bear!" He looked around, walked to the other side of the ridge and saw the bloody remains of the Indian, Coyote, and Bear made a snarling grin as he laughed and said, "Well, that's what happens when a wolf takes on a coyote!" He looked at the stretched-out form of the gray wolf, lying motionless near the mutilated body of Coyote. Bear turned away and started back to his horse to return to his camp. He thought about the grulla of Tate and wondered where it might be. He walked around a bit, couldn't find the grulla, and went to his own horse to leave.

When a horseman of any worth ties off his horse, it's never with a secure knot but a loose tether, so that if necessary, the horse can pull free and find his way home or to safety. When Coyote neared Shady, the horse was alarmed and jerked away from the Indian's touch, and when the Indian pursued, the horse pulled free and trotted away. Coyote's intention was to chase the horse down after they dealt with the lookout, but such was not to be, and Shady had found refuge in a distant clump of juniper.

Bear wasn't concerned with horses, he even let the Indian's mount go free as he started his return to the camp of his men. Without the need for cover, he pointed his horse directly west toward the camp by the feeder creek. He would get the men together and they would start for the meet-up with the renegades and plan their attack on the wagons. He grinned at the memory of his vengeance on Tate and the thought of his yet to be delivered revenge on the men of the wagons. He chuckled to himself at the thought of what he considered delicious vengeance.

CHAPTER TWENTY-ONE
ATTACK

MARK SLID THE HORSE TO A STOP AT THE EDGE OF THE WAGONS and quickly stepped down all the while hollering for the men. "Hurry! Hurry! They're comin'!"

"Who's coming," retorted Gertrude Pickett, "an' quit'chur hollerin', ever'body can hear you!" She stood wiping her hands on her apron and began adjusting the straps on her bonnet. The sudden arrival of Mark startled the woman and she fidgeted trying to regain her composure while the others came to the edge of the wagons.

Henry Hyde stepped forward and said, "Alright, what is it?"

Mark was breathing heavily and took a deep breath and began, "Well, me'n Tate was watchin' their fires an'," he was interrupted by Hyde. "Fires, what fires?"

"The campfires!" answered Mark. "The campfires of the Injuns!"

"What Indians?" asked Hyde.

"Well, if you'd quit interruptin' him, maybe he'd tell ya'," interjected Lucas.

"Alright, go on," mumbled Hyde.

"Well, we saw two different bunches. One way off to the north and Tate thinks that was Bear and his bunch. Then there was several fires together to the east, and he thinks that was Injuns. We waited till light and sure 'nuff, it was Injuns alright and he sent me to warn y'all."

"Warn us of what? Are they gonna attack?" asked Hyde.

"Well, we don' know for sure, but he said we needed to get ready in case," answered Mark, nodding his head all the while. "He said we need to be sure to put a lookout up on top there," nodding his head to the top of the mound, "an' to watch the notch."

The men had prepared well for the probability of an attack. The animals were tethered near the river to graze in the tall grass and two men were sent to start bringing them into the deep cut on the south side of the mound. Other men pushed one of the wagons aside to make a gateway for the animals while others began positioning the women and checking the weapons. Mark volunteered to take one of the spots on the rock that would enable him to fire down on any attackers as well as to watch the notch. The men had determined who would be placed where and one of those shooters would be Mark and the other would be Jason. The two girls would be hidden higher up and would also be armed. Their purpose was to sound a warning to the boys and shoot if necessary.

The highest lookout would be Hank, the young son of Henry Hyde, who was quite proud to be chosen for such a responsibility. Although part of the reason for him being chosen was his father thought he would be safer up there. He was cautioned by his Pa that what he did could save the entire wagon train. The only weapon that could be spared was a pistol. Although the use of the percussion cap was gaining popularity, it was not real common, with most still using the flintlock. However, the pistol used by Hank was a

.38 caliber percussion cap pistol. He hefted the pistol, liking the feel of it in his hand. His father had taught him how to shoot and load the weapon and had given him enough powder and bullets for six reloads.

The men and women were stationed around the half-moon of wagons with ample goods for cover placed underneath and between the wagons. The two ridges to the sides of the notch would be manned by one shooter and a reloader, with each man strategically protected by well-placed large rocks that made a firing pit. Every shooter had placed powder horns and patched bullets alongside the ramrods or wiping sticks and those with smooth bore shotguns were equally prepared. Before they took their places, Edmond Bowman called them all together to join hands and to lead them in prayer. As the amens were said, everyone quickly went to their places and prepared themselves. The young people scampered up the smooth rock to their designated places and Hank scurried to the very top. He carefully crested the top, belly down and no sooner lifted his head and he dropped back down, turned and spoke just loud enough for Charly Bowman to hear, "They're comin'! The Injuns are comin'!"

She spoke quickly and told him to count how many and which way they were coming. Then she turned and hollered to Jason, just below her and said, "They're coming! The Indians are coming!"

Jason shouted to tell the others by the wagons and turned back to see Charly looking to Hank. She relayed his message, "Looks like twelve or so, and they're all coming around that-away," motioning to the west end of the mound. The men expected them to come from that direction, with the river to their east, the only way they could come from that side would expose them as they crossed the river. Throughout the wagons, the click of cocking hammers was heard, and low mumbles of additional prayers were muttered. Hyde spoke to Lucas positioned behind the nearest wagon and said, "Hope that boy's right about the number. If that's all there is, we should do alright."

Lucas responded, "Just don't go gettin' excited. Take your time, space your shots."

The enthusiastic Hank was determined to be the best lookout ever and when the Indians moved to the west end, he scampered across the top of the mound so he could look down on them. It was farther than he thought and when he neared the top, he saw the Indians already starting around the south side. He saw they had split into two groups with one moving close to the rock and the other moving toward the river. He counted and realized there were some missing and counted again. He had a sudden thought and scampered back to his original lookout, just in time to see two Indians dismounting and starting up the notch. He dropped down, spoke just loud enough for the girls to hear and told them there were two coming. Hank went to his hidey hole and waited, nervously fingering his pistol. He knew the girls would be ready and they probably told Jason and Mark, but what should he do? He decided to wait until they passed his hideout and hoped the girls would stay hidden.

The two youngest warriors, Badger and Crooked Arrow, had been given the task of climbing the rock and working their way down behind the wagons. They were eager for the fight as this was the first fight for Crooked Arrow and only the second one for Badger. Badger assumed the lead and whispered orders to Arrow as the two climbed the rock. The smooth stone was hard granite but in places the surface was somewhat sandy, and their moccasins slipped and made a whispering noise that they were certain anyone stationed to guard would hear. When there was no response, they breathed easier, thinking their way was clear and they could come on the wagons undetected.

Hank could see the wagons below and the wide span of grassy flats between the wagons and the river. He saw the six Indians riding single-file to the edge of the river, readying to attack. Nearer to the monolith, five more were moving toward the narrow ridge that protected the wagons. As he watched, he heard the whisper of the moccasins on the stone and he hunkered down behind the boulder that was his cover. The wide crack in the mound behind the boulder gave him additional cover and he hugged the near wall, afraid to be seen by the two climbers. Hank heard the two whisper as they neared, and he waited, thinking their shadows would pass close enough to be seen as they started down the cut.

He saw nothing, but another whisper of moccasin on stone told Hank they had passed. He slowly raised up and saw the backs of the two warriors. The Indians were slowly making their way lower, knowing any sudden movement would give them away as they moved from rock to crack. They were no more than twenty feet past Hank when he stepped from behind his rock and took aim at the nearest warrior. His hands trembled as he held the pistol out in front, high enough to take aim and he tried to squeeze the trigger as his dad taught him, but he had no strength. The pistol shook, and his eyes watered, and he lowered the weapon, wiped his eyes with his sleeve and pulled the heavy pistol up to again take sight. The Indian was now a couple of paces farther, but the boy began to squeeze. Suddenly the pistol roared, and a cloud of white smoke belched to follow the lead ball from the muzzle. The targeted Indian stumbled forward, hitting his fellow warrior as he fell.

Hank dropped his hands and stared at the fallen Indian, not seeing the other warrior turning and bringing his bow up with nocked arrow towards him. But the roar of a rifle startled both the warrior and hank as the impact of the bullet in his side dropped the Indian where he stood. Hank looked up to see Charly Bowman slowly lowering the rifle in her hands. Her face was as white as the smoke that still hung in the air from the discharged rifle and Hank stared at the girl with wide eyes, realizing both of them had just killed an Indian.

The shots from high up on the mound triggered the attack from the Indians by the river and the screaming of their war cries brought the attention of those by the wagons back from the rock. The girls' mother, Sylvia Bowman, was tasked with reloading for her husband. She was afraid of shooting a rifle, but now worried about her girls, her hands trembled as she readied the balls, patches, powder and ramrod.

Russell Prescott and his wife, Rebekkah were stationed atop the finger ridge that protected the west flank of the wagons. They were just below the crest, with Russell hidden with a large stone so he could watch the approach of the group of renegades that sought to come from alongside the mound. As the larger group charged toward the wagons, those stationed inside the perimeter of the wagons held their fire until the order of Henry Hyde. When the attackers came within just over thirty yards, that command was given, and a wall of lead greeted Crazy Elk and his warriors. The massive roar of the simultaneous firing of nine rifles reverberated across the valley and the explosion of smoke hid the attackers from the wagons and vice versa.

When the attack came from the river, those that were approaching from behind the finger ridge started to climb the ridge but the sudden appearance of Russell Prescott and the thunder of his .60 caliber flinter together with the belch of smoke, startled the climbers and sent one to his back with a red blossom of blood in the center of his chest. The nearest warrior believed the white man's weapon was now empty and he tried scampering up the sandy surfaced slope. As he was grabbing for a handhold, Prescott cut loose with his second rifle and saved the warrior the need of climbing the rock, as he left a trail of blood sliding back down the slope. Prescott dropped and handed his second rifle to his wife, accepting the reloaded one. He rose to search for another target but the slowly fading cloud of smoke showed no Indians remained, except for those unable to flee.

The rest of the Indians jerked their horses around and fled under cover of the smoke. But as the cloud slowly dissipated, the shooters at the wagons were disappointed to see only two bodies left behind.

IF IT WASN'T for the thunderous roar of the shooters from the wagons, Bear and company probably wouldn't have known of the attack. With the wagons on the far side of the mound and Bear and company a few miles away, the sound of a few shots would not have carried. But the combined blast was more easily heard. Bear reined up and asked Sully, "Did'ju hear that? Was that gunfire?"

Sully turned his head to lend his good ear to the distance, shook his head and said, "I dunno, but it did sound like a explosion or sumpin'."

Bear turned back to the others, "Did'ju hear that?"

"Hear what?" asked Gimpy.

"Sounded like gunfire ta' me. I'm thinkin' them crazy renegade Injuns done hit them wagons." He paused as if to listen some more, then hollered, "Come on, let's get a move on. I ain't lettin' them redskins take them wagons!" He kicked his horse to a gallop and changed the direction to a direct route to the mound, foregoing any meeting up with the Indians at the river crossing.

THE GIRLS and Hank had watched the battle from their lofty perches, and as the Indians dispersed, Charly turned and told Hank to get back up on top and watch for any more Indians. He turned and scampered back to the crest. There were no more attackers climbing up and he scooted back to lay on his belly and watch the flats beyond. He quickly grew restless and decided to go to the higher part of the mound to see if he could see where the band of Indians had gathered. Thinking he might need to see what they were doing so he could sound a warning, he scampered to the highest point and dropped to his belly. The curvature of the mound prevented him from seeing the group of Indians that were gathered at the base of the monolith and arguing about what they should do next. Their voices carried up, so he knew they were there, but he couldn't understand their language. He pushed himself up and moved to return to his lookout, but a movement in the distance caught his eye and he dropped back down. Riders were coming and coming fast judging by the cloud of dust they were dragging. He slid back a mite and waited until he could see better, and the big figure of Bear was unmistakable. Hank immediately rose to a slight crouch and dropped slightly over the crest to hide from the coming riders as he scampered back to his lookout.

"More riders comin'," he motioned as he called out to Charly. "An' I'm sure it's Bear and his men!"

The wide-eyed Charly waved to show she heard and understood then turned to relay the alarm to Jason in his trench just below. He stood and hollered down to the wagons, "Hank says more riders are comin' and it looks like Bear and his men!"

Henry Hyde waved his recognition and understanding and turned to Lucas as he said, "We coulda gone all day and not have them come." He started to say more but another message came from above, "Four men!"

Lucas said, "Well, even with four more, that's still less'n they started with. We done in six countin' them two up top, an' I'm thinkin' we mighta wounded some more."

"Well, you keep a look out, I'm gonna walk around an' make sure the folks're alright. Might need to encourage 'em a little," said Henry as he stepped away from the wagon. "We need to be ready, I don't think them injuns'll wait very long 'fore they attack again," he added as he started around the wagons.

CHAPTER TWENTY-TWO
RECOVERY

His face felt wet, was it blood? Every part of his body hurt. He tried to move, tried to open his eyes, nothing was working. Something warm and wet across his face, trying to open his eyes. He struggled to move his arm, but it was too heavy. Breathe, breathe, hard to breathe. There it is again, that warm and wet sensation. Must be bleeding, everything's dark, maybe dead. But dead can't hurt this much. A sliver of light, blurred, bright, hurts. Wet. The dirt in his eyes ground into his eyelids, bringing more pain. But he knew he had to fight, that warm, wet feeling again. What was that? Then the whine, almost a question, forced him to fight the pain and open his eyes. Just a slit with one eye showed sunlight, but no, more of a shadow.

The long wet, warm, tongue slobbered across his face and he opened his eyes to see a blurry patch of gray fur. He tried to shake his head to clear his vision, but his motion was limited, and the pain seared deep. He blinked his eyes and the vision cleared somewhat to reveal more gray fur and then that deep red wet tongue crossed his face again. Tate finally realized it was Lobo licking his face, trying to revive him.

Tate grunted, tried to speak, heard the whine of the wolf and felt relief wash over him like a warm bath. He struggled to move and to speak, but all he managed was a moan that elicited more licking and whining from the wolf. Lobo began to dig away the dirt and rocks that had partially buried Tate, letting the man finally free his arm to help.

As he fought against the rocks, gravel, and dirt, he was able to lift his head and get a good look at Lobo. A dark red crease made a furrow across the top of the wolf's skull and dried blood showed on both sides of the bullet made trench. Tate realized a wound like that would have done in most animals, but Lobo was tough and mean and hard-headed, which had served him well. A short while later, Tate was able to sit up, but instantly leaned back. He was very near the precipice of the cliff. If he slid any further, he would surely plummet to the bottom where he would never be found and would be good for nothing but fish food.

He began scooting up the slope, warily watching the precipice as if it was in pursuit. When he was about eight feet away, he rolled over to his belly to look up the steep side of the narrow ravine. Lobo was beside him and he looked at the wolf and said, "Well, boy, looks like we got a bit of a climb." Together, man and wolf clawed and crawled slowly up the wall of the ravine. Each movement bringing rock and dirt down, but the pain forced him to move. Moving and looking like a four-legged spider, and stopping often, he finally crabbed his way over the lip of the steep sided ravine. He flopped over on his back and sucked air, every breath bringing agony to the side with the broken ribs. He stared at the clouds, trying to gather his thoughts.

His first thought was weapons, he reached to his belt, tomahawk gone, then to the holster, pistol gone. He felt the knife at his back, and thought, *well, that's somethin', but wait, maybe I can find my hawk and my pistol, if Bear didn't get 'em.* He struggled to his feet and looked around. He walked over to the big flat rock he had used as his promontory point, remembered placing his spyglass down, and walked around, spotted the scope and bent to retrieve it. *Now, I was standing about there when Bear knocked my pistol, thataway.* He looked in the direction where the pistol should be, walked nearer searching the ground and all around, he moved back and forth in an arcing motion, searching. *There! In those rocks!* He walked over and picked up the pistol, dusted it off, tested the action, and grinned. He turned back towards the rock and caught a glimmer of light off of something, looked closer and saw the hawk. He went to retrieve it and was disappointed to see the handle was split but it could be used in a pinch. *Maybe I can wrap it with rawhide to reinforce it.* He was feeling well heeled and looked around for Lobo. He was nowhere to be seen. *Now, where'd that wolf get off to?*

Feeling a little faint, Tate staggered to the flat rock and sat down, dropping his head to his hands. He felt the knots, cuts, dried blood, swollen eyes, and realized he had to tend to his wounds. *Gotta clean 'em out 'fore they get corruption or infected. Maybe I can get down to the river, below the canyon. Can't go too far, that Indian camp. Wonder what happened to Shady?*

He didn't want to put it to words but nagging in the back of his mind was his concern about the wagons. Knowing Bear was in the area, he was intensely conscious the wagons were in danger, but there was no way he could get to them to warn them, not without a horse anyway.

He heard movement and brought his head up, a little too fast, and dizziness and blurred vision came on him. He stretched his arms down to the rock beside him to stabilize himself before he toppled over. He saw movement, blurred though it was, and squinted his already swollen eyes to try to make it out. The gray form of the big wolf was trotting toward him in his lumbering gait, moving silently, and right behind him was the blue-grey grulla, Shady. Tate let a grin cut his face and winced with the pain, but the joy of seeing his beloved companions chased the pain away and he stood to await his friends.

He dropped to one knee and wrapped his arms around Lobo's neck and hugged the beast, bloody hair and all. He stood and put his arms around the neck of Shady, hugged his neck and patted the side of his head and behind his ears. He was grinning and chuckling and said to the pair, "A man ain't never had better friends than you two!" He looked to see his bow still in its sheath under the left saddle fender, walked around to the other side and saw the butt of his Hawken protruding from the scabbard. *How can a man be so lucky? Just a while ago I thought I was dead, and now I'm with my friends and outfitted too.* He lifted his eyes heavenward and said aloud, "Thank you, Lord. I know this is your doin', and I'm mighty thankful. Oh, and while we're talkin', how 'bout takin' care o' them folks with the wagons?"

Tate tightened the cinch on the saddle, gave everything a once over, and stretched to put his foot in the stirrup and was stopped by the pain. He dropped his head to rest on the edge of the seat of the saddle, took a deep breath, and with the determination needed, made a slight hop, put his foot in the stirrup and swung aboard, wincing all the while. Once seated, he grabbed at his side and said, "I'm gonna have to bind that up, can't have no ribs pokin' into muh lungs or nuthin'."

The light of day was fading fast and Tate had little light to tend to his wounds. With Shady ground tied and grazing at river's edge, the man walked into the water, followed by Lobo, and sat down to allow the cool water to soothe his miserable body. He splashed water on his face and head, massaging the bumps and cuts, reached over and playfully rubbed the wet wolf behind the ears and rubbed the dried blood from his fur. He examined the crease as best he could. There was no fresh blood, so he knew the wolf would be fine. Now if Lobo could do the same for him, that would help, but he felt around, knew some of the cuts now with the dried blood gone, were bleeding and would have to be tended. But he enjoyed the refreshing coolness of the water and soaked a while longer.

He waded from the river, wiping the excess water from his buckskins, and walked to the side of Shady. He would have a cold camp, taking some pemmican from his saddle-bags and settling on his bedroll by the alders. Lobo had given his usual shake to rid himself of the water and rolled in the grass for his final rubdown. He stretched out beside Tate, accepting the throwntidbits of pemmican and the friends lay back for a much-needed rest. He knew he was close enough to the mound that if there were any sounds of attack, he could hear it and with nothing but silence around him, he determined to wait. Tate knew any help he could give the wagons would be better rendered in the morning about first light, and he also knew he needed to recuperate from his beating before he could help anyone.

His restless night brought him fully awake before the first light of dawn. With his eyes accustomed to the dim light of the moon and myriad of stars, he checked his weapons, cleaning them and replacing the cylinder of his Paterson with one of fresh loads, then carefully reloaded the first cylinder with five new loads of the .36 caliber balls and caps. He used the wiping stick with its screw tip to remove the load from his Hawken and reloaded the rifle with a fresh load as well. He had allowed a long strip of rawhide to soak in the backwater of the river and now retrieved it, wiped it clean and began carefully wrapping the handle of his hawk to reinforce the wood. He knew the addition of the rawhide, after it cured, would make it even stronger than before.

Satisfied with his preparations, he brought Shady close in and began gearing up for the day.

He didn't know what to expect, but with no sounds of a battle, he hoped for the best. It was by the light of the rising sun that he rounded the west end of the mound, noting the abundance of tracks going both directions. When he came in sight of the location of the wagons, he was surprised to see nothing. As he rode closer, he was cautious and observant, looking all about for any sign of renegades or others. Yet, all was quiet. He heard the chuckle of the Sweetwater, a chattering song of a meadowlark came from the willows by the river, and the whisper of the wind seemed to carry a somber message of death.

As he rounded the point of the finger ridge that had protected the wagons, he was brought up short by the signs of a battle. He sat mesmerized by the scene before him. The remains of a partially burned wagon with charred bones of what had been bows that held the white bonnet arched over the burned wagon box that sat askew, with one corner on the ground and the rest held by partially burned wheels. The carcasses of two mules lay beyond, with crows and magpies picking at the remains and a coyote snatching at the hind quarters for mouthfuls of meatfrom the bloated carcass. Turkey buzzards were arguing with a bald eagle over the remains of what had been a paint pony of one of the attacking Indians. Other carrion were busy at the bodies of men scattered among the grass of the flats between the site of the wagons and the river. The smell of death and rotting flesh filled Tate's nostrils and he pulled his neckerchief to cover his nose.

He stepped down from his mount and dropped the reins to ground tie Shady and with Lobo at his side, he walked among the battle-scarred remains of the massacre to try to understand what had happened. As he moved into the middle of the notch that had been the refuge of the wagons, he spotted a cluster of graves by the finger ridge to the south and walked closer. Six graves marked by crude crosses lay with parallel mounds of dirt and rock. With nothing to identify one from the other, Tate could only assume these were graves of some from the wagons. He dropped his head, muttered a short prayer and lifted his eyes to look around. There were blood trails on the rock ridges, and turkey buzzard showed bodies lying askew high up on the notch of the mound. He counted the bodies that had been left for the animals and numbered nine. With nine Indian bodies and six graves the tally could only be described as a massacre. Tate hung his head thinking this was his responsibility. He believed he had failed the families of the wagons, and he led Shady from the scene of the slaughter and swung aboard to follow the wagons and do what he could to make up for their loss.

As he followed the tracks of the wagons, he also noted the tracks of the surviving attackers following the trail that took them back to the north around the west end of the mound. He tucked that information away in the event he would need it in the coming days. After he found the wagons and understood what had happened, he would set out to do what he could to balance the scales of justice.

CHAPTER TWENTY-THREE
RETURN

BEFORE LEAVING THE BIG MOUND THAT WOULD EVENTUALLY become known as Independence Rock, the girls and Jason and Mark, using hammers and rocks, etched their names and the date on the big monolith. Those were not the first names to be inscribed and seeing the others, they prompted the young people to leave their marks as well. As they stepped back and looked at their handiwork. Hank read, *Charlotte and Cassandra Bowman, Mark Hillyard, Jason Pickett, and Henry Hyde Jr., July 6, 1840.* They had just finished when a call from below bid them come to the wagons. There was still enough light to make a few miles and Henry Hyde had even suggested they might keep moving well after sunset. They were anxious to be as far from this place as possible. Although they didn't think the remaining renegades and outlaw whites would try again, they all agreed they wanted to distance themselves from the site of the massacre.

They had only been on the move less than an hour when Weston Hillyard, the scout for the day, rode up and stopped the wagons. After he conferred with the lead drivers, they started to move again and soon found out they would have to cross the river and resume the trail on the south side. Wes had told of the foothills, mostly rock, that loomed near the river and made it impossible to stay on the north side. It was an easy gravel bottomed crossing with gentle sloping banks and the wagons easily made it through the slow-moving water.

Mark had been given the responsibility of rear guard and he followed at a distance of about a mile. With the extended absence of Tate, the men had assumed he had been taken either by the Indians or by Bear and his company. It was totally out of character for Tate to be away from the wagons for that long and especially when he and Tate had scouted the camps of the attackers. Tate had told Mark he would stay behind and do what he could, but he had apparently failed. Mark was thinking about the time he had spent with Tate and the many lessons learned and he wanted to emulate the man as much as possible.

Keeping his rifle primed and ready, he lay the weapon across the pommel of his saddle and kept his eyes moving, searching for any sign of danger. With dusk slowly giving way to the encroaching darkness, Mark looked to the rocky hillsides and saw a dark cloud rising. His first thought was smoke, but as the cloud switched directions, he realized what he was witnessing was the exodus of a vast number of bats, making their way into the night for their feast of the evening. He smiled at his mistake and with gentle knee pressure, urged his mount to move back out on the trail of the wagons.

It was a clear night and the indigo canopy was bedecked with millions of pinpoints of light, some glimmering, others staring with brightness for the travelers below. The sliver of moon, a little fatter than the night before, did little to add to the brightness, but it did add. As his eyes grew accustomed to the night, Mark revelled in the mysterious beauty of a landscape punctuated by dark shadows and magical images made by the blended figures of stone and trees. As he searched the surrounding terrain; the river beside him gurgled on its way to its meeting with the larger North Platte. Mark's concentration was dimmed as he listened to the night's sounds of cicadas and nighthawks. He had learned to enjoy the night, after the many scouts he and Jason had been on, and with the lessons learned from Tate. When he thought he saw movement in the dark shadows, he did as Tate had taught, and looked to the side, letting his peripheral vision catch any real movement. Seeing none, he continued to follow the trail of the wagons, stopping often to search the backtrail for any sign of pursuit.

The wagon train did as they had become accustomed under Tate's leadership and stopped just after midnight. They would make a temporary camp for a few hours rest for both animals and man, then start again with first light. By early afternoon, they circled up on a grassy flat between two of the many double-back bends of the Sweetwater. Mark was sent across the river to a bald knob that would give a good point to view of the surrounding area and he could search for any sign of trouble. He staked out his horse, loosened the cinch, and climbed the bald knob for his look-about. With nothing in sight but a distant herd of pronghorns, he leaned back and covered his eyes with his hat, set on taking a snooze in the afternoon sun.

When the sun became unbearable, Mark sat up and looked around. It was crowding late afternoon as he looked down at the river, saw what he thought was the younger group, so he went to his horse and started toward the others. When he approached, Jason hollered, "Howdy Mark. Come on and join in, we're catchin' fish for supper!" Mark grinned as he gigged his horse into the water and made his way to the opposite shore. He flipped the reins over the horse's neck and loosened the cinch, giving the horse the freedom to fill up on the tall green grass. He walked over to Jason and listened as the young man began, "Charly and Cassie are using poles an' worms. I was too until Hank started doin' better just usin' his hand. Come on, I'll show ya." He led Mark to where Hank was belly down on the bank with one arm dangling in the water. Jason lowered his voice and said, "See, where the river makes a wide bend, it cuts out under the bank and the fish like to lay in there waitin' for bugs an' such. He stays here so his shadow doesn't hit the water, then slowly puts his hand down, like this," and he showed his arm extended with his hand forming a shape r like a cup, "and slowly moves until he feels a fish. Then ya slip you're hand up under, slide it forward to the front fins right behind the gills, then slowly tighten, just enough so you can slip it forward and bring him up by havin' hold right there. Now, watch him, he's good at it. I've got a couple, but look at that stick yonder, he's got maybe ten nice trout already."

Jason had no sooner finished his description when Hank brought up another nice trout, twisting and flipping its tail, trying to get away. Hank tossed him into the grass, stood and chased after it, picked it up and stuck the end of his stringer stick in the gill and out the mouth and looked to Mark and said, "Go ahead and give it a try. It's fun!" Mark gave it a go, lost one, caught one, and surrendered to Hank as the best fisherman. The five youngsters proudly paraded into the circle of wagons with their stringer sticks loaded with trout.

They had harvested almost three dozen nice sized trout that would make a good meal for everyone. The women were tickled for the change and dug out the cornmeal to roll the trout in and prepared their big cast iron skillets to fry the feast. Everyone was enjoying their meal, talking and laughing, when a voice came from beyond the wagons asking, "Ya got 'nuff for one more?"

Everyone looked around, trying to figure out if it was

one of their number or a stranger. But they all visibly relaxed when Tate stepped across the dropped tongue of the wagon and into the circle. His face still bore the cuts and bruises and swollen black eyes that told of his fight, but they recognized the outfit and his voice and were relieved to see the man. He was peppered with questions and welcomes that came so fast all he could do was hold up his hands and say, "Uh, if it's alright with everyone, how 'bout I answer all your questions after we eat?" Laughter broke out and everyone returned to their plates and continued with the festivities. With the return of Tate, it had become almost a celebration but as the meal was finished, everyone gathered around to hear his tale and to share their stories.

He sat on an upturned nail keg and told about his beating at the hand of Bear and his slow return from the dead by the tongue of Lobo. There was little more to say than, "I'm sorry I didn't make it back in time, but, believe me, I tried."

Henry Hyde started, "Well, let me tell ya' what you missed, and you folks," motioning to the rest of the crowd in the circle, "jump in wherever you feel like it." He began with the warning given by Mark and their preparations, and their repelling of the first attack. "But when they came back, that Bear and his crew was with 'em. We didn't see him at first, cuz they went around the east side and come acrost' the river. When they come at us from that way, we wasn't expectin' it and it was them that shot Charles and Hettie Heaton. The Websters were at the first wagon on that end, an' that's when Matthew went down."

"So, it was the white men that shot those folks?" asked Tate.

"Yeah, but then the darnedest thing happened. The rest o' them Injuns that started to attack us, turned on Bear an' his bunch, an' they was fightin' each other. I think we killed a couple, maybe three of the renegades, an' they killed two o' the white men."

Hyde was interrupted by Lucas, "Don't forget the fryin' pan!" and everyone laughed.

"Oh, yeah, while all that was goin' on a couple Injuns jumped 'tween a the wagons, but Gertrude there saw 'em comin'. She met one when she slapped him right on his face with her cast iron skillet. You heard o' the Flathead Indians? Well, she made that one into a Flatfaced Indian. He was stretched out purty as you please, looked like he run into a brick wall. Gertrude there stood over him shakin' that skillet an' the other'n turned tail an' ran on back where he came from!" Everyone laughed as they looked at a stern-faced Gertrude that was doing her best not to join in the laughter.

Henry continued, "Then the rest o' them renegades, why they gathered up the rifles an' such, even those of the Heaton's and then they took off chasin' Bear an' that other big guy and Gramps, you know, the white-haired fella that was Bear's sidekick. The other big fella had an arrow stickin' outa his back and Gramps horse had one floppin' in his rump. Don't know how far they'll get."

"So, those six graves, that was the Heaton's and Matthew and the other white men?" asked Tate.

"Well, no, ya' see, after Matthew went down, he got a blast right in his face, his woman, Lydia, was so tore up, she just wailed and hollered. The other women tried to comfort her but she was hysterical and talkin' 'bout how she couldn't live without him. Then she just snatched up his pistol and shot herself in the head, 'fore anybody could stop her. We buried 'em side by side. So, four o' them graves were our folks, and the other two were the white men. One of 'em was the one with the club foot, but we never saw the other'n before. We didn't see no need o' buryin' the Indians, we figgered they'd come back an' get 'em after we left. Did they?"

Tate slowly shook his head and said, "The only thing that came after 'em was buzzards, crows and coyotes."

The families had jointly decided to return to the usual routine of traveling during the daylight hours only, camping at night. The irregular schedule had been difficult on them all and they were anxious to return to the normal hours. Everyone turned in for the night, hoping to catch up on some lost hours of rest, knowing daybreak would rouse them all too soon. All were anxious to distance themselves from the scene of the massacre although they knew it would require more than distance and time to heal the wounds of remembrance.

TATE STOOD beside Shady and spoke to Henry Hyde, "Henry, I just don't think Bear and his bunch will give up that easy. They been followin' us for weeks, just because he was mad at losin' his job and wantin' to get even with me. And I'm sure part of his reason was to rob you folks and pay you back. Those things haven't changed, and now with the added insult of losing some of his men and havin' to face up to them renegades, he's gonna be madder'n a wet hornet. So, I'm goin' back yonder and put a stop to him, one way or the other."

"Well, I understand what you're sayin', but we'd rather have you with us."

"I know, and I promise I'll be back as soon as I can. You just keep followin' the Sweetwater and as you get to the mountains, you'll see where the trail cuts off and makes it o'er South Pass. You just follow that an' it'll take you into one o' the purtiest valleys you ever did see. You might wanna settle down there, but if not, the trail's purty easy to follow on west till you find what you're lookin' for, but hopefully I'll be back 'fore then," explained Tate.

"You've still got some supplies in the wagons, what do we do with 'em?" asked Hyde.

"If I ain't back by the time you top off on South Pass, just cache 'em on the northside under some trees, blaze the tree, an' I'll find 'em. But I've got some of 'em with me. I'm takin' one of my pack-horses and some supplies since I'll be gone a few days."

The men shook hands and Tate mounted up, reined his mount around and started back on the trail toward the big monolith. He would pick up the trail of Bear and the others where they crossed the river in their flight from the Indians. Maybe he'd be lucky, and they would all kill each other. He chuckled at the thought.

CHAPTER TWENTY-FOUR
TRAITOR

THE HORSES SPLASHED THROUGH THE WATER SENDING WAVES crashing and men slapping leather in their panic to flee the battle. The plan of Bear and his men had quickly been thwarted by the combination of entrenched and determined farmers and the renegades that betrayed them. Bear spotted the grinning face of Hoots through the grey/white cloud of gunsmoke and he barely had time to flinch away from the arrow from Hoots bow. When Bear saw Gramps take an arrow in his back and the horse of Sully stagger from another, he knew the entire band of renegades had foiled their plan and turned against them. Bear led the way through the river and across the Sweetwater, beating his horse with the barrel of his rifle, trying to get more out of him. He had glanced over his shoulder as his horse mounted the river-bank and saw some of the Indians gesturing their direction. He knew they would soon be in pursuit.

Gramps was hunkered over the pommel of his saddle as his horse clawed its way up the slippery bank, and once on the flat, it shook the water free. Gramps kicked his heels into the ribs of the horse, watching Bear's horse kicking dirt as they fled with no thought of Gramps or anyone else. Gramps wrapped the saddle straps around his wrists as he fought for some relief from the arrow protruding from his back. As he looked through the flying mane, another horse came along-side, and Gramps saw the big figure of Sully slapping leather trying to catch up with Bear. Neither man had given Gramps more than a glance, believing the white-haired man was as good as dead.

A RIDGE of rock rose before them and Bear reined around the north end, pulled up and stood in his stirrups to see if they were being chased by the renegades. So far, there was no one after them, but he noted the only ones with him were Gramps and Sully. He had seen Gimpy take a bullet to his neck from one of the farmers, right before that same farmer tumbled from his perch on the rocky ridge thanks to a bullet from Sully. Bear knew his first shot had killed the farmer by the wagon, but he couldn't tell which one it was, but he laughed at the shocked expression on the man's face when he grabbed at his chest and his hand came away bloody. He had been surprised to see a woman on the ridge with that farmer, Heaton, but he had also seen Gimpy cackle when he shot her. Bear searched their backtrail for any sign of the only other white man, Moose, the friend of Sully, but he apparently had taken an arrow or a bullet and wouldn't be coming.

"Ya gotta help me, Bear," pleaded Gramps. "Get this . . . arrow outta me," he struggled to talk, "I can't ride with it in me like that," he groaned as he turned his head to look at Bear. There was no compassion on the whiskered face of the big man, only disgust and anger.

"We cain't stop now! Them Injuns'll be comin', if'n you cain't ride, we'll just hafta leave ya!" he growled.

Sully's horse limped closer to the others as the big man

leaned back to see how bad his mount was hit. He swung down and walked back to look closer and saw blood pulsing from the wound of the deeply embedded arrow. Sully pulled his pistol from his belt and put the muzzle close behind the horse's ear and pulled the trigger. The blast made the other horses jerk in surprise, but they didn't shy away. Sully looked at Gramps and the arrow sticking from his back, saw where the blood was spreading across his back and down his side. He looked up at Bear and both men knew what was to be done. During their short stop, Bear had been reloading his rifle and pistol, and after putting his rifle back in the scabbard, he started to put the pistol in his belt, then on second thought, handed it butt first to Sully. Without a word, Sully primed the pan, lowered the frizen, cocked the hammer, and with one hand jerked Gramps from the saddle and as he hit the ground, Sully shot him in the side of the head. He started to hand the pistol back to Bear but was stopped by an upraised hand as Bear said, "Reload it!"

Bear looked up from Sully toward the scene of the battle, said, "Mount up! Them Injuns's comin'!" Bear jerked the head of his horse around and slapped leather as he kicked the horse to a full gallop away from the small ridge of rocks and fled across a stretch of sage covered flats toward a distant ridge. Sully was close behind but eating the dust from Bear's fleeing mount. The two shots had told the renegades the location of the white men and prompted them to give chase.

HOOTS LED two other renegades to give chase after the fleeing white men. While Hoots wanted vengeance on Bear, the others were just after plunder, particularly the weapons of the white men. When they rounded the first mound of rocks and spotted the dead white man and the horse, Hoots found himself alone in his pursuit as the others had stopped to strip the corpse of his gear. When he realized he was alone, Hoots reined up and returned to the rocks and the two warriors stripping the white man. One was standing, waving a rifle in the air, showing off his prize. The other had tucked the pistol in his belt and was taking the prized scalp of white hair. Hoots, or Owl that Walks, joined the others, searching the body and the gear for any other prizes of plunder. Hoots grabbed a knife and scabbard, saddle bags with nothing but some smoked meat and some smelly long-johns. They looked up as Flat Nose and Crazy Elk rode up beside them, and heard Flat Nose say, "We go after them." The five renegades started on the tracks at an almost leisurely walk.

"Whar we goin'?" called Sully as he and Bear had slowed their horses to a canter. Both men continually looked behind them, fearful of seeing the entire renegade band closing in on them. Bear twisted around and seeing no one close behind, he slowed his horse to a walk and motioned directly before them to a long low ridge with a singular cut. "Thar! Through that cut yonder, an' we'll head southwest after that. Thar's a ridge of sawtooth mountains with lots o' timber and plenty o' water. If we git away from them Injuns, we'll rest up thar."

By the time the timbered ridge came into view, their horses were well lathered and in need of rest. They had already crossed several dry gulches, but the sight of greenery was a big relief as they neared a small creek in a grass and brush covered narrow valley. Before dropping into the valley bottom, they reined up and searched for any sign of pursuit on their backtrail. Seeing none, Bear nudged his horse off the slight embankment and into the narrow stream. The horse needed little encouragement and began to drink deeply. Bear had dropped off and buried his own face in the water, but quickly came to his feet and pulled the head of the horse up and said, "Whoa there, boy. Take 'er easy, don't wanna go gettin' yourself all bloated up. We'll rest a spell," he encouraged as he led the horse away from the stream and put his nose down to the grass. Without any hesitation, the animal cropped a mouthful and lifted his head to survey his surroundings as he munched on the welcome graze. Sully had done the same with his horse and the two animals stood together, very familiar with one another, as Gramps' horse and Bear's had traveled many trails together.

The two big men sat down in the shade of some tall alders and reloaded their rifles and checked the loads in the pistols. Sully looked at Bear and asked, "So, now what?"

"What'chu mean?" answered Bear.

"I mean, what're we gonna do now? With only two of us, we'll be lucky to get away from them renegades, but then what'chu got in yore mind?"

"I'm still goin' after them wagons!" declared a vengeful Bear.

"Just us?" asked Sully, a bit incredulously.

"They still got ever'thing we want, money, women, guns, so we go get it," declared Bear.

Sully shook his head and said, "Them farmers done killed some o' our men and a whole bunch o' them Injuns, an' you want us two to take 'em on?"

"Yup, we just do it different this time. They ain't got no scout cuz I done kilt him, an' when they're all spread out, we can jus' pick 'em off, one or two at a time. Then we move in an' take ever'thing we want!" proclaimed Bear. Every hour that had passed since they attacked the wagons, Bear had been stewing in his anger and planning his revenge. There was nothing that would stop him from getting what he wanted, and he was determined to get his vengeance and enjoy the doing of it.

Sully stared at the scowling visage of the man who looked

the part of his name and dropped his head as he said, "It just might work. Course, if it don't, we prob'ly won't be alive to complain 'bout it."

CRAZY ELK and Flat Nose had agreed on their plan or strategy. They knew that white men, when they saw no one giving chase, would begin to feel safe and slow down, even camp for the night. Flat Nose sent one of his men back to their camp for the women and others to follow them. When Hoots had first visited their camp, three warriors had been out on a hunt and would have followed the band and joined the camp by this time. If they made good time as they followed, they would have these three additional warriors when they chose to take the white men. They had no doubt they would catch the white men and would see if these men knew how to die well. But even if they did not, Flat Nose knew the men had weapons that would make his band stronger. They had lost some of their number, but with the white man's rifles, it would be easy to get other warriors to join their band and soon their village would be strong, strong enough to take other white men's wagons or even to wage war against other villages of their enemies. But first, they must capture these two men that were running like cowardly antelope.

LOBO SCOUTED WELL IN FRONT OF THE SLOWER MOVING TATE and his grulla. Tate's broken ribs had been dealing him fits even with the restraints applied by the well-meaning Gertrude. The easy rambling gait of Shady made riding as tolerable as possible, but the kicks and beating from Bear had left considerable marks, cuts and bruises. When Tate stopped for a short break in the late morning hours and knelt at the edge of the backwater pool of the river, he scooped up wateras he knelt on one knee, using the butt of his Hawken to steady himself at river's edge. When the water stilled, he saw his reflection and shook his head at the sight. Black eyes, swollen cheek and jaw, cuts on his forehead and eyebrow, were just the visible injuries. As bad as those looked, the pain came often and stabbing from his broken ribs.

When Gertrude saw him wincing in pain as he ate his supper the night before, she took over the tending of his injuries and paid special attention to his ribs. As she examined the bones and bruises, it was all Tate could do to keep from crying out, she wasn't the most tender in her ministrations. When most would describe Gertrude as 'matronly',

Tate thought the only apt description would be 'manly.' He thought she was more of a man than most of the men on the wagon train, and he didn't know any of the men that would dare to cross her. When she brought out the contraption she was determined to use to bind up his ribs, he was quick and adamant about his protests, but they fell on deaf ears as she instructed her husband and Lucas, the big blacksmith, to hold him down while she tended to him. She had stripped him down to his bare nothings and Lucas held his hands together over his head and Jeffrey held his legs, but neither of them could keep a straight face nor keep from laughing while they restrained him. Gertrude was as serious as a narrow-minded Preacher as she slipped one of her old corsets over his head and down to his rib cage before she began cinching it tight. Before she tied it off, she let a rare smile cross her face as she snickered at the thought of this mountain man in a woman's corset.

She stepped back and said, "Now them corset stays'll keep you sittin' up straight and thatcorset'll keep your ribs secure. Now, don't go gettin' in no hurry to take it off, unless you want one o' them ribs pokin' your lungs. If that happens, you'll drown in yore own blood, an' that'll be mighty painful. I don' know how you managed to make it this far, only by the grace of God, I reckon. An' it's a good thing there was a woman that was woman enough to have one o' them things big enough to do the job. Course, that weren't me, I ain't wore one o' them things in ages. Don't need 'em no more." She stood with her hands on her hips grinning at the men as they fought to keep a straight face.

Tate ran his hands along his ribs and grudgingly admitted that Gertrude was right, and the contraption had made it easier and less painful as he rode. He put his weight on the Hawken as he stood up and led Shady to stand by a flat stone that was just the right height to help Tate step into the stirrup and slowly swing his leg over Shady's rump as he prepared to get back on the trail. He had guesstimated it would take a full day to get back to the site of the battle and pick up the track of Bear and any of his men. Depending on where they went from there would determine how long it would take for him to overtake them and settle things.

Dusk was just beginning to dim the light when Tate started across the Sweetwater following the obvious trail of Bear and his followers. When he crested the other bank, Tate stepped down to examine the tracks and to give Shady and the pack-horse a chance to shake and maybe snatch a couple of mouthfuls of fresh grass. It was easy to see that Bear and his men were followed by the renegades. Based on what the farmers had told him, Tate believed the renegades were chasing after Bear, not traveling with him. Because of the overlying tracks of the renegades, he couldn't tell how many of Bear's men were with him.

Tate looked around and realized he was on the ground where there were no handy rocks nearby to make his mounting easy. With the contraption, he refused to call it a corset, restricting his movement, he knew he would have to walk a ways until he found something to aid him in mounting. Lobo didn't understand why Tate was walking and leading Shady, but he trotted along beside him, happy for the company. Tate looked down at the healing crease across Lobo's head and said, "Look's like you're mendin' pretty well, boy. It's a good thing Gertrude didn't see that, or she'd probably wrapped your head in a pair a bloomers or sumpin'."

They were still walking when he rounded the north end of the formation of rocks that had been the first cover taken by Bear. The remains of the horse and the body of Gramps had been picked at by carrion, but Tate still recognized the tufts of white hair. He had thought of making their camp on the lee side of this mound, but the stench of rotting flesh and the presence of turkey buzzards, coyotes, and even a badger, convinced Tate to continue his search for a stepping stone. Fortunately, it was just a short distance before a cluster of rocks gave him the help he needed and once back aboard Shady, he moved out in the direction of the rocky ridge with the cut. He had thought about trying to bury Gramps but knew his contraption would greatly limit his movement and he decided to forego the deed.

He had stopped for a meal and a rest for both him and the horses and chose to just loosen the rigs on the animals in favor of resuming the trail after a short snooze. It was a clear night and the moon was waxing full as it rose over the eastern flats. The milky way painted the black sky with a carpet of stars and a great horned owl asked its question of the wilderness bringing Tate awake and reminding him of his trek. Still struggling with his contraption, he had to roll to his stomach, push himself up on hands and knees, and struggle to his feet with the aid of his Hawken for a crutch. He tightened the cinches on the horses' rigs and with the aid of a gray weather-beaten log, mounted Shady. He motioned for Lobo to scout ahead and nudged Shady to follow.

The big moon cast a long shadow of the far sawtooth ridge that loomed in the darkness before him when Tate was stopped with Lobo standing crosswise in the trail. His stance told Tate there was trouble ahead, so he reined up and began looking around for a place of good cover to stop for the rest of the night. He pushed farther into the thicker timber and found a suitable clearing. He stripped the gear from the mounts, picketed them on some grass and rolled out his bedroll nearby. He would trust the horses and Lobo to be vigilant as he tried to get some sleep with the consarned contraption restricting his movement.

The smell of smoke brought Tate fully awake. There was just a hint of early light trying to filter through the thick pines as Tate carefully scanned the clearing by moving only his eyes. His hand clasped the grip of the Paterson as he looked and listened. He saw the horses standing hipshot and undisturbed and Lobo was awake and watched him move his eyes about. With none of the animals concerned, Tate relaxed and rolled to begin his struggle to stand, this time using Lobo as his aid. He looked around, saw nothing, but knew he wasn't mistaken about the smell of smoke. There was a camp nearby, and he decided to scout around on foot to see if he could find out who his neighbors were.

With Lobo at his side, Tate chose to move through the timber, taking advantage of the carpet of pine needles to quiet his movement. He found a game trail that paralleled the crest of the ridge and stayed in the black timber. Tate was well experienced at stealth in the woods, having stalked game in the Missouri woods as a youth and spent time with Red Calf, his Osage friend, as they tried to stalk one another. Suddenly, Lobo dropped to his belly, a low growl growing deep in his chest. Tate lowered his hand to the wolf's neck, whispered, "Easy boy," and knelt beside his friend. He searched the trees, dropping low to see below the lowest branches of the spruce and fir, breathing deep to smell the smoke of the early morning campfires. He waited, listened, unmoving, watchful for any movement of guards or scouts or others just moving into the woods for their morning business. Rising to a low crouch, he slowly moved forward, more silent than the whisper of the morning breeze through the branches.

Staying well behind a large spruce, he watched the movement of the camp before him. He was surprised to see women working to erect two hide lodges and others shaping brush huts and lean-tos. He had crossed a trail late last night and knew this was the village of the renegades. Their women had moved to join them. He wasn't close enough to get a count of how many warriors, but the activity seemed to show more than the few that had been trailing Bear and company. He slowly backed away and began working his way back to his camp. Now he had some thinking to do, he could no longer follow the trail of the renegades as they pursued Bear, not with the camp in the trail. He couldn't drop out of the timber and move across the flats, he would be certain to be seen. The ridges were too steep and thick with timber to move above the camp and around. Perhaps his only option would be to cross over the ridge and parallel the trail on the opposite side and come back through farther beyond. But first, he was going to have some smoked meat and water for his cold camp breakfast, then decide.

BEAR AND SULLY RODE UP FROM THE CREEK BOTTOM TO THE highest knoll among the hills that bordered the creek. That promontory provided a view of the entire area. With prairie flats all around, the men saw no sign of any followers. Bear motioned to the foothills to the northwest, "The Sweetwater and the trail them wagons'll be takin' run along them hills yonder. If'n we head off down thataway," motioning toward the wide cut between some low rising hills on the north and a long ridge to the south, "I'm thinkin' we can catch 'em in that grassy flat."

Sully looked where Bear was pointing, then scanned the area nearby. When he noticed the creek they had stopped by actually forked and they were on the peninsula between the forks, he said, "Ain't that Pete Creek," motioning to the forks. "Ya know, the one whar ol Pete McGee and his mule got buried in the bog an' all they found was his hat?"

Bear looked around, laughed, and said, "By gum, I think it is! They said ol' Pete used to take a drink, give one to his mule, take 'nother'n, and so on till both him an' the mule was so drunk, neither one o' 'em could stand up. They musta both been drunk when they went into that bog."

"We ain't got much light left, how 'bout we head to that strip o' green yonder, looks like another crick, might find us some fresh meat an' make a good camp," suggested Sully. Bear looked where Sully pointed and nodded his head as he gigged his mount toward the green. The sun was gone, and twilight guided the two to the small creek where they made their camp for the night.

"THEY ARE by the small stream that moves like a snake below the pillar of red rocks," reported Cloud Dancer, one of the two scouts given the task of following the white men from the battle for the wagons. "Two men, both big, one with many whiskers. Both have guns and more. They look for wagons beyond river, there," pointing to the distant Sweetwater.

Flat Nose looked to Crazy Elk, giving a slight nod of acknowledgment to the younger leader of the renegades. Elk had formulated the plan to allow the white men time to believe they were not followed before the renegades would take them. Both men were familiar with the location described by the scouts and together considered their opportunities. Within moments, they agreed upon a plan to overtake their prey and sent Cloud Dancer to tell the other warriors to prepare.

WHETHER IT WAS arrogance or stupidity or a combination of the two, Bear and Sully believed themselves safe from discovery by the renegades. As is true with most perpetrators of evil deeds, they thought themselves smarter and better than those that opposed them. Even to the point of believing themselves nigh unto invincibility, they believed themselves safe and without need of any caution that would demand they be watchful and observant to the point of having one on guard throughout the night. If anyone dared to attack them, their size, brawn and smarts would allow them to overcome anyone that would presume themselves able to defeat them.

The warriors noted the brash attitude that allowed Bear and Sully to drop into a deep sleep, evidenced by the snores of the men as they unconsciously wandered the halls of dreamland. The snorts and growls made the watchers think of a battle between a bear and a mountain lion, each trying to outdo the other. With the only light coming from the fading stars of early morning, the stealthy warriors slowly approached the outstretched figures of Bear and Sully. Both were partially covered by blankets with their heads on the seats of their saddles. While two warriors stood at their feet, arrows at full draw pointed at the throats of the sleepers, two other warriors took the rifles that lay beside the men and handed them off to others. As the rattling snores continued to mask any other sounds, the same two warriors drew their knives and simultaneously pricked the throats of the two sleepers, bringing them instantly awake.

"Wha . . . uh . . . uh . . . " muttered Bear as he came instantly awake, and stopped himself from moving, feeling the knife at his throat and seeing the other warrior ready and even anxious to send an arrow into his middle. Sully simply groaned as he too woke, and slowly raised his hands overhead as he warily watched the two warriors that held him under their weapons.

Flat Nose stepped forward to stand at the feet of the two big white men. Bear recognized him as the leader of the renegades recruited by Hoots, or Owl that Walks. Flat Nose said, "Up, now, you will come, and we will see if you are a warrior or a coyote that whines and runs away."

"Whatchu mean? Wha'doya' think you're a doin' anyway? You got no call to do this!" snarled Bear, mustering up his usual bravado that normally intimidated anyone that dared to face him. But Flat Nose did not answer as he motioned to his men to make thestand and to bind their hands and legs. When Bear stood, two warriors grabbed his hands to pull them back, but Bear started to fight back. He knocked one of the men down and as he growled at the other fighting to free himself from the warrior's grip. A sudden blow to the back of Bear's head with the flat of a tomahawk knocked him to his knees, causing him to slump forward and a second blow brought the blackness of unconsciousness that dropped him face down in the dirt.

Sully struggled with those that sought to bind him, but seeing Bear so easily overcome, Sully surrendered to the two that held him. Within moments his hands were bound behind him and he was made to mount his horse that was brought to his side, devoid of any gear save a bridle. When he was astraddle of the horse, his feet were bound together with a long rawhide under the belly of the animal. Bear was laid belly down over the back of his horse and the Indians bound him with a long rawhide from his feet, under the horse's belly, and around the neck of the big man. Sully looked at the unconscious form of Bear and knew the man would have a rough ride to wherever they were taken.

Sully fought with his bonds. But as the horse found his footing to mount the slight bank of the wide arroyo that held the narrow creek, he was more concerned about keeping his balance to stay aboard the mount. The war party of rene-gades was silent as the dim light of early morning chased the stars from the sky. Sully counted the number of warriors, all

the while thinking of any way he could escape. The ten renegades were well armed, and most had rifles obviously taken
during the battle with the farmers and from those that had
ridden with Bear.

The warrior that led Bear's horse held to the rifle that
Sully had carried for several years, a .60 caliber Kentucky
style rifle that he had converted from a flinter to a percussion. He hated to see it in the hands of an Indian. That rifle
had served him well and like many men of the mountains, he
had named it. Choosing the name of his first sweetheart,
Penelope, he referred to his rifle as "Penny." And to see Penny
in the hands of an Indian raised the ire of Sully as he thought,
*I'm gonna get that redskin and use Penny to put a ball right 'tween
his eyes.*

Sully was still fighting, unsuccessfully, with his bonds and
contemplating his revenge when the war party came to their
camp just within the edge of the black timber of the
sawtooth ridge. They were greeted by a handful of women
that had cookfires flaring and pots hanging as they prepared
the morning meal for their men. Bear was the first to be
taken from his horse, growling and shouting at the men that
pulled him to the ground. He tried kicking at the Indians, but
he was grabbed from behind and drug toward the trees at the
edge of the camp. Sully watched as Bear was lifted to his feet
and with two warriors standing before the big man with
lances ready to be thrust into his midriff, Bear's legs were cut
free. But new strips of rawhide were tied to each ankle and
pulled to trees that stood about ten feet apart. Then his
hands were freed and stretched to the same trees. When the
warriors were finished securing the big man, he was spread-
eagled between the two trees, with his bonds tight enough to
prevent any movement. When Bear continued to shout and
growl, one warrior stuffed his mouth with a wad of buckskin

and wrapped a wide strip around his face and neck to keep it tight. Even Sully was relieved when Bear was silenced, but when the warriors came for him, he shook his head as he knew he would be spread-eagled just like Bear.

CHAPTER TWENTY-SEVEN
DISCOVERY

"WELL LOBO, I THINK WE'RE GONNA HAVE TO GIVE IT A TRY. This ridge is too steep and rocky to go over the top, an' it'll take us too long to go back and circle around it, an' we for sure and certain ain't gonna try to make it across them flats. Why, if we went thataway, them renegades would spot us in a heartbeat and then we'd be done for, so, as I see it, we gotta sneak around above 'em. What'chu think, huh?" Tate looked at the expectant eyes of Lobo who had listened to every word, then reached down and ran his hands through the thick fur at the scruff of his neck. "So, does this mean you agree with me?" he asked as he rubbed the big wolf behind his ears. Tate was sitting on the big grey log and Lobo was sitting on his haunches at the feet of his friend, enjoying the attention. Sometimes it seemed as if the wolf did understand what Tate was saying. At least he understood when the man gave a verbal command or a simple motion of his hand and Lobo instantly responded. If he didn't understand every word of the conversation, he understood the sentiment and emotion. With his usual open-mouthed grin, lolling tongue and wagging tail, Lobo showed his willingness to go with his master anywhere.

Tate lifted his eyes to the falling darkness, searching for the rising moon and scanning the skies for clouds. What he was about to do he knew would be one of the most dangerous undertakings he ever attempted. To try to sneak by a camp of renegade Indians that had attacked the wagon train and tried to kill every white man and woman there, was tempting fate. These were outcasts from their own villages, men that had shown themselves completely without scruples and willing to kill anyone to get what they wanted. If he were to be caught, there would be no negotiations, no wrangling for mercy, they would kill him and probably do it in the most gruesome way they could devise. But he had to locate Bear and whoever was with him and do whatever he could to keep that murderer from another attempt to take over the wagon train. That's the least he could do for those that had become his friends and who trusted him to get them safely to their promised land. He had already failed them once when he didn't get back to help repel the attacks by the renegades and Bear's bunch. He couldn't fail them again.

He stroked the neck fur of the wolf, "Well boy," lifting his eyes to the few stars that began to show themselves, "I'm thinkin' we'll move out in about an hour or so. Folks usually sleep their soundest round about midnight and the few hours after. You know, in the darkest of the night. I dunno if them renegades will have any kinda guard out, but we gotta assume so. I know you'll move quiet, but I hafta get Shady an' the packhorse through real quiet like. I'm hopin' that game trail I saw a little earlier will stay in the thicker timber, high up, an' away from their camp. Guess we'll find out soon enough, though."

He scooted down on his bedroll, and with his head on the

saddle seat, he reached over and laid his arm across Lobo, "Let's get us a few winks in 'fore we take out, alright with you boy?" He rubbed the top of the wolf's head and rolled to his back to stare at the stars. *Boy, if my Ma and Pa could see me now, sleepin' in the woods near a renegade Indian camp and talking to a wolf. Why, Ma'd have a conniption fit! Course, Pa'd just laugh though.* After a time in prayer, he tried to snooze, but he never fell into a deep sleep, and when he judged it to be close to midnight he rolled from his blankets and geared up his horses. The moon was bright, sky cloudless, and stars abundant, as he waved to Lobo to take to the trail.

He rode with his Hawken across the pommel and his head on a swivel, constantly searching the thick timber for any sign of movement or indication of the renegades' awareness of his presence. The thick carpet of pine needles worked to his advantage and the shuffling gait of the horses was almost soundless. Tate could tell by the smell of smoke they were passing above the camp and as near as he could judge they were over fifty yards higher up the rocky hillside of the sawtooth ridge. The thick timber was impenetrable in the darkness and he could only get glimpses between the trees maybe ten yards or slightly more. He knew the thicker the trees, the more any sound of his passing would be muffled.

Lobo was moving with his loping trot about ten to fifteen yards ahead of the horses, but he suddenly stopped, frozen in place as he slowly lowered his head and raised his hackles. Tate slipped from his saddle and stealthily moved up behind the wolf, also searching the trees and the trail. Coming towards them were two wolves, one slightly ahead of and to the side the other, but both in the same stance as Lobo. The lead wolf was almost completely black and his eyes blazed orange as he curled his lip to show his fangs. The second wolf was marked similar to Lobo and was smaller than the black. Lobo was both taller and heavier than either of the two, but both had battle scars showing they were not newcomers to the trail by battle. They stopped, staring at the big wolf before them, both snarling but the growls could barely be heard. Lobo's lip was curled, and his big fangs dripped with saliva of anticipation. His forehead wrinkled, making his eyes almost squint and even though Tate was behind him, he knew Lobo's eyes were flaming as well. Lobo lifted one foot, moving it forward as if in a challenge, put it down and lifted the other, showing he was ready to fight.

When the black wolf first saw Lobo, he lowered his head and assumed the stance of attack. But when Tate walked up behind him, the black wolf's eyes caught the sight of the man and showed confusion. A slight turn of his head assured him his mate was with him, and the black stared back at Lobo as if to say, "Another time," and turned from the trail to trot into the timber. Lobo's eyes followed the two wolves, and when they had disappeared, he visibly relaxed. He looked back at Tate, and started walking on the trail, giving the man time to remount and follow.

As they moved out, Tate looked heavenward and whispered, "Thank you, Lord. That coulda been a real mess. Wolves don't know how to fight quiet an' I'd probably had to shoot one and that woulda brought the renegades and . . . well, You know. So thanks." He dropped his eyes back to the trail to see a glimpse of grey fur disappear around a bend. The rest of their passage above the renegade camp was without incident and all, animals included, seemed to relax just a bit when Tate felt they were far enough past the camp to move down the slope. His plan was to try to make it to one of the stream-bottomed ravines that cut into the flats below before first light.

As they neared the tree line, Tate reined up and stepped

down. He dropped the reins to ground tie Shady and with Lobo at his side, he walked to the edge of the trees to survey the flats by the light of the moon. Nothing was moving, and the usual night sounds were undisturbed. He searched for a likely ravine and saw a small cut that seemed to widen farther into the flats. Most of these gullies were storm run-off carved, and the floodwaters clawed their way to the Sweetwater that was the lowest point in the valley. If he could make it to that ravine without being spotted, it would give him cover all the way to the Sweetwater. If Bear and his companions were shadowing the wagon train as he thought, their tracks would have to cut across that ravine and if they didn't, that would mean he had gotten ahead of them as he hoped.

He looked at what would be his chosen path one more time, and started to turn back to his horses, when movement caught his eye. He searched the tree line to see a line of mounted renegades, about a half mile back, coming from the trees and moving across the flats. They were traveling slowly, quietly, and Tate knew they were intent on some kind of attack. That could only mean they knew where Bear and friends were, and they were going after them. But Tate knew there was nothing he could do, even if he wanted to, not one man against what looked like a dozen or so warriors. He would just have to wait it out and see what happened. Maybe they would solve his problem with Bear and company.

He moved back into the trees, searching for a likely spot to hold up until the Indians were done with their mission. He soon found a suitable clearing, and tethered his horses, loosened the cinches on their gear and grabbed a handful of smoked meat from his saddlebags and made himself comfortable. Lobo stretched out at his side and the two enjoyed a morning snack. Tate was thinking how good a cup of coffee would be but decided against any fire that might alarm any scouts from the Indian camp. *Maybe we'll just take a snooze.* "Yeah, that's what we'll do boy, let's take us a good snooze. Now, don't you go sleepin' too sound, I wouldn't want them renegades to catch us sleepin'," he admonished the wolf, patting his head and sharing his meat.

CHAPTER TWENTY-EIGHT
ALARM

MARK'S HORSE WAS KICKING UP THE DUST AS THE YOUNG MAN lay along his neck, encouraging the animal for more speed. Mark slapped leather as he took a quick look over his shoulder, fearful of seeing a band of marauding Indians on his tail. But the glance showed no pursuit, and he used the long reins to smack the horse on his rump, begging him not to slow down. At first sight of the wagons, he sat upright waving his free arm and shouted, "Injuns! Injuns!" He couldn't tell if they heard or understood, but he never slacked his pace.

Weston Hillyard's wagon was in the lead and his wife Ruth was the first to spot their young scout and son, Mark, as he galloped toward the wagons. "Wes! That's Mark, and he's trying to tell us something. Oh, my word, what is he shouting?" She stood up, anxious to see her son, but fearful of whatever his warning was about. As he neared, she shouted, "What is it? What are you shouting?"

"It's Injuns, a bunch of 'em!" responded Mark.

"How many? And how far back?" asked his father, Weston.

"I dunno, I just seen their tracks! But I think there was at least a dozen, maybe as many as twenty!" rattled the young man.

Two other wagons had pulled alongside the first and Henry Hyde asked, "What's all the ruckus?"

Mark looked at the leader of the group and said, "Injuns, sir, Injuns!"

"Indians? How many and where?" asked Hyde.

"I'll start the wagons circlin'!" shouted an excited Russell Prescott. He and his wife were in the wagon on the other side of Hillyard's and he was known for his nervous anxiety, especially when it came to any danger, or even a perceived problem.

Henry Hyde hollered across to the man, "Hold on! Just wait a minute." He turned back to Mark and asked again, "How many and where?"

"Well sir, I didn't see them, just their tracks! But, I'd say there were somewhere 'tween a dozen an' twenty," answered Mark, a little sheepishly.

"You only saw tracks?" asked Henry, somewhat incredulous.

"Yessir, but Tate said if there's tracks, they ain't far!"

"Are you sure they were Indians and were the tracks fresh?" quizzed Henry.

"Yessir, none o' the horses were shod, an' the tracks was fresh enough, all right, cuz the pebbles were still damp," assured Mark.

"The pebbles were damp?" asked Henry, confused.

"Yessir, Tate showed me 'bout trackin' an' he said when a track is made, often the horse or whatever, kicks some pebble over in the track an' that shows the underside. You know, where the pebble was stuck in the ground. And if'n that's still damp an' the sun ain't dried it out, that means they passed within about an hour," explained Mark.

Henry looked at the young man, thinking about the

young man's explanation and warning, then decided. He stepped up on the springboard seat and looked at the surrounding terrain, pointed to the north toward a cluster of hillocks and hollered to Russell Prescott, "Lead the wagon's over there an' have 'em circle up. Looks like there might be a spring thereabouts and we'll just make camp to be on the safe side."

Prescott nodded his head and hollered as he slapped reins on the rumps of his mules, "Gittyup mules!" and pulled on the right reins and started the mules toward the designated location. Henry motioned for the other wagons to follow, then dropped down to the his seat and spoke to Weston Hillyard, "Go ahead and follow the others over there, I'll be right behind. Mark, you go back along the trail and keep a lookout till I send someone to spell you. Keep your head down, an' if you see 'em comin', be sure to light out and warn us!"

Mark looked at the man, relieved they were heeding his warning, and answered, "Yessir!" as he reined his mount around to backtrack his own trail. When he saw the tracks, he was following the wagon trail that had charted their course since Fort Laramie. It took them through the cut between the smaller mountain ranges and now followed the Sweetwater just to the south of mountainous terrain that was mostly large stone mountains that appeared as singular massive stones and interspersed with rock strewn hills dotted with juniper and piñion trees. Mark had crossed over the Sweetwater to the north side wanting to find a high point promontory to get a better view of the distant flats and the direction of the Sweetwater valley.

He had gone no more than a mile from the river and was approaching a ridge with a rocky point that resembled a stone face when the tracks caught his eye. Those tracks had rounded the rocky point and pointed toward a notch between the line of stone covered hills to the north. From what he had been told by Tate, Mark thought these might be the peaceful Cheyenne, but he also remembered Tate talking about the Arapaho and he wondered just what tribe were these Indians? And were they in any danger?

When he arrived back at the rocky ridge, he tethered his horse at a cluster of juniper and climbed the stone covered slope to top out the ridge. Once atop, he took out the spyglass loaned to him by Henry Hyde and bellied down on the granite knob and began his scan of the country beyond. His first concern was the Indians and he searched the valley that disappeared between the rocky knolls, the west one having a bald dome that rose as the highest point on that formation and the nearer formation with a higher point. He saw greenery in the bottom of the notch and assumed a creek came from there and followed the far formation and eventually met the Sweetwater. Even though he saw two small herds of antelope, there was no sign of Indians. He tried to follow their tracks with the scope but was unable to follow the trail but about a hundred yards, the tracks grew too faint to follow further.

He relaxed and sat up to look around. Behind him he saw a peak of the solid stone hill that looked like it had been split by some giant with an axe. The cut of the peak was further enhanced by the crease in the mountain that came toward his perch and was littered with greenery in the bottom, not enough to indicate a stream, but there was grass and brush that showed at least moist soil. As he scanned the formations he was amazed that the hills appeared as if they were solid rock, very little vegetation or loose soil, but the rock was marked as if the Creator had left His fingerprints on each stone.

Mark was continually amazed at the dryness of the country, even though a river twisted its way along the edge of these mountains, the distant plains were basically brown. He thought of the area that had been their home near Saint Joseph, Missouri. Land that was green and abundant with everything growing in the fertile soil. Sometimes the problem wasn't getting things to grow but getting the right things to grow and keeping other wild growth away from the fields. Here, it seemed the only thing that grew willingly was cactus. But he liked this wild country, the vastness of it, the challenge of it and even the people that lived here, red and white. They were a strong people that met the challenge of the land and made their homes here. He breathed deep as he thought of the wild land and as he looked around, he thought of how much he had come to love this land, it fit him, and he had never felt that before.

Mark turned back to scan the distant valley and the trail used by the Indians for any sign of their presence or their return. Seeing none, he searched the entire horizon for any sign of danger, and was pleased at the absence of any life, other than the antelope, and some deer walking to the river. With dusk fast approaching, he felt there was nothing of concern and decided to leave. He stood and slipped and slid down the rocky slope to his horse, mounted and started back to the wagons.

HENRY HYDE and Lucas Colgan greeted Mark as he returned to the wagons. He gave his report of not finding the Indians and that he believed they had gone from the area, much to the relief of the two men. They would relay the report and he started for his family's wagon, but was intercepted by Jason Pickett, the young man that shared Mark's responsibility of scouting. As they shared the events of their day, Jason said, "Great! We've had Indians behind us, and now we've got Indians in front of us. What're we gonna find tomorrow?"

"That my friend, will be up to you. You're gonna be

scoutin' ahead, an' I'll have your easy job of trailin' behind. But hopefully, Tate'll be catchin' up soon," answered Mark.

Jason replied, "Yeah, I hope so. Then he can do the scoutin' an' we can get back to serious business, you know, with the girls!"

Mark laughed and said, "You'n Charly are gettin' kinda serious, ain't you?"

"What's wrong with that? You an' Cassie have been steppin' out just as much as we have," retorted Jason.

"Yeah, but, you know, I've been thinkin', thinkin' 'bout makin' my life kinda like Tate. I'm gettin' to where I like this country," motioning with a broad sweep of his arm, "and if the mountains are ever'thing Tate says, I think I'm gonna like them even more. And I think Cassie's intent on havin' a farmer for a husband, not a mountain man."

Jason looked at his friend, wondering if he could really stay in the wilderness and said, "Hummm, I dunno. Charly says Cassie's pretty smitten with you, an' if that's so, it shouldn't make any difference where you are, mountains or farm."

"Well, that may be, but I ain't sure the mountains are any place for a woman anyway," answered Mark.

The manly discussion about the ways of women was interrupted by the two girls returning with buckets of water retrieved from the small spring fed stream. When Mark and Jason saw them, they quickly offered to carry the buckets for the girls, who just as quickly relented. Whispered invitations were exchanged before they parted and both couples had agreed to meet after supper.

"WHEN DID you decide you wanted to stay in the mountains?" asked Cassie as she looked at Mark. They were sitting side by side on a broad boulder just apart from the wagons. The full moon gave a glow to the shadowy flats and the broad milky way arched overhead.

Mark let out a long sigh and said, "Well, I dunno really, I was just thinkin' 'bout it today when I was out on the scout. I was up on this bald knob of a rock and lookin' around and just thought how much this country has kinda grown on me. I guess the thought of bein' a farmer never did have much appeal for me. When I talked with Tate about the mountains and what he's done, it just seemed right, like something I've been lookin' for and didn't even know it." He clasped her hand and looked at her, "I know you had your heart set on settin' up a new home, having your own place with lotsa kids runnin' around, but . . . " He let the thought drop and dropped his eyes as well.

Cassie sat silent, looking at the big moon overhead, and glancing back at Mark and back at the heavens. She stirred and turned to face him and began, "Mark, I like you, maybe even love you, but what I want is to be happy with the man I believe the Lord has for me. It really doesn't matter if it's on a farm, in a cabin in the mountains, or even on a ship at sea. If I'm certain that God has chosen that man for me, then I'll be happy," and she giggled a little, "whether or not there's a bunch of kids running around or not. And if He shows me that you're that man, then Mr. Pickett, you'll be stuck with me, even in the mountains!"

Mark grinned as he looked at the smiling Cassie and said, "So, I guess that means we need to be checking in with the Lord to see if we are s'posed to be together, that right?"

Cassie nodded her head and said, "Ummmhummm. 'Cause if the Lord's not in it, we shouldn't be either."

THE WAGONS WERE on the move with the first light. Long shadows preceded them as the rising sun was directly behind them and the rugged hills beyond beckoned. With the roadway following the south bank of the Sweetwater, the slight rise in the terrain gave them an overlook of the twisting river that wound among the willows and alders in the bottom of the valley.

Less than an hour on the trail brought them around the rocky mounds and the split-rock formation that Mark had told them about. As Edmond and Sylvia Bowman, now in the lead wagon, stretched out their mules on this leg of the trail, Edmond thought he saw something unusual on the rounded point of the hill just beyond the river. He did a double take and caught his breath, which made Sylvia look to her husband. When she saw the expression of alarm, she turned to look in the same direction. There on the skyline of the long rocky ridge, were three mounted Indians; two holding lances and war shields, the third with a rifle, the butt of the stock on his thigh. They were a quarter of a mile away, but easily seen as they were sky-lined. Edmond remembered Tate telling the men that usually they wouldn't see the Indians, but when they did, it would be for a purpose. Either the Indians were giving a warning or simply showing their presence. Either way, it called for caution on the part of the wagon train. Edmond drew back on the leads of his mules and waited for another wagon to draw near. When two wagons came up, one on either side, Edmond asked, "Did you see?"

THE BOY THAT STOOD STARING AT THE SPREAD-EAGLED BEAR was about eight summers of age. He had been playing with a hoop, chasing it through the village with a couple of other children, but when he saw the captives, he stopped to stare. Bear glared at the child, tried to growl but his gag limited his noise to a stifled mumble. The boy let a grin paint his face and bent down to pick up a rock. He hefted it, looked at the big hairy man, hefted it again, then let it fly with all his might. The glancing blow to Bear's forehead elicited another stifled mumble and a wicked glare at the boy. The boy laughed as he picked up another stone. He hefted the stone, looked to the village and called for his friends. Two others, a boy and a girl, close to the same age ran up to the first boy and he motioned toward the captive with his chin, hoisted the stone again, and threw it at Bear, hitting him on the upper shoulder. Bear pulled at his tethers, tried kicking at the boy, tossed his head back and forth, and did his best to shout. The children laughed and ran away.

"They teach 'em young, don't they?" asked Sully. Bear

glared at his fellow captive and tried unsuccessfully to speak through the gag. "How long ya' think it'll be 'fore them renegades come back after us?" inquired Sully. Bear did his best to shrug his shoulders to answer, but the tight bonds, now digging into his wrists, prevented any movement. They had been bound for about two hours, long enough for the Indians to take their midday meal and confab together about the captives.

"THEY SHOULD DIE AND DIE SLOWLY!" proclaimed Owl that Walks. "This man wanted to massacre the whites on the wagons, but it was our people who were massacred! He said we could take them easy, but they fought well, and our warriors died. Both of these whites should die a hard death!"

The other warriors had gathered in the circle to consider the fate of the captives. Many nodded their heads at the demand of Owl that Walks. Crazy Elk rose, "After our first attack, this man said we could take them with his help and we would have many rifles, but his men were no good. The only rifles we have, we took from his men. This man lies and should die!" Again, many heads nodded and the mumbling of agreeing comments was heard.

Flat Nose remained seated and spoke up, "I agree with our brothers. They should die, and they should know our anger. The village will do this, they too have felt the loss." His declaration was met with several loud outbursts and war cries, as all rose to retrieve their weapons, anticipating the coming torture. When Flat Nose said the village would do this, the people knew the method that was chosen, and it would be a long and painful death for the captives.

"HERE THEY COME," said Sully as he nodded his head toward the village. Led by the rock-chucking boy, it appeared the entire village was following. As they neared, the boy bent down to pick up another rock and without hesitation, he threw it at Bear, but missed the big man. The boy shrugged his shoulders and walked along the path in front of both captives, others following. The women all carried switches of willow or alder and as they passed by, each took a swipe at the men, but never hitting them. The passing branches made both men duck away but they were relieved when none connected. The women were followed by warriors, youngest first, and all were armed. Several glared at the captives, but none made even a threatening gesture. When all had passed, Sully said, "Now, what was that all about?"

The villagers had filed past into the trees, but silently returned to pass behind the captives. The first realization that Sully had was when one of the women slapped the back of his neck with her willow switch. Almost at the same time, another woman hit Bear in the same way. But then the entire group stopped behind the men and two warriors approached with knives. Sully squirmed and twisted his head around, fearful eyes with big whites, thinking they were going to be stabbed from behind. But instead, the two warriors used the knives to cut the buckskin tunics from the white men, leaving them with only their union suits covering their torsos. But the warriors cut those around the waist and completely bared the men from the waist up. Several of the Indians spoke and pointed at Bear and his torso and upper arms covered with thick black hair. The black bear was revered by some Indian tribes, but these were renegades, and although some gave thought to the appearance and name of the big man, all were still eager for his torture and death.

Again, the boy led the procession, but this time even the

rocks thrown by the children found their marks and blood began to show. The women were vicious as their repeated blows turned the flesh of Sully red and made Bear squirm to free himself. The younger warriors, armed with knives and lances, were careful with their thrusts and jabs, barely breaking the skin, but also bringing blood. None of the wounds were deep, but the blood came from foreheads marked with welts and cuts, and the cuts on their torsos now flowed with crimson. The older warriors stopped and stepped back from the captives to watch as the women brought dry sticks and twigs and stacked them between the legs of the captives. Both men looked at the women, down at the wood, and realized what was about to happen. Bears eyes were wide with fear, and then he narrowed them with hate as he glared at the leaders standing before him. He muttered through the gag, obviously making threats and taunts as he glowered at Owl that Walks, the one he had called Hoots, who stood in the middle of the leaders.

Owl grinned, "Now, Bear, we will hear you growl!"

Both men knew Indians respected bravery, and both had heard tales of those that whimpered and begged when undergoing torture and had the torment lengthened and worsened. Although they had not conferred with one another to agree on their reactions, they were both determined to show no weakness. But when the wood was stacked between their legs, their resolve to be strong was tested and both wavered. Sully, without a gag, began to curse and beg the renegades to kill him. Bear could only stare and squirm, the gag was held in place with the rawhide band around his face.

Sully saw the line forming again and said to Bear, "Get ready, they're comin' again!" The boys had exchanged their rock throwing for their small bows and arrows, the women had swapped their switches for knives. As the procession passed, there were shouts and war cries as everyone drew blood. The warriors cut deep, but not into the organs, and the arrows pierced flesh but not the torso. Bear and Sully struggled against their bonds and screamed, or tried to, with each cut. But when the fires were lit, both men wet themselves and as the flames licked flesh, Sully screamed. The smell of singed and burning hair permeated Bear's nose and his eyes flared with fear as he realized that was his hair burning.

———

TATE'S SNOOZE was interrupted by a wet tongue and dripping slobbers from the mouth of Lobo trying to rouse his master. It was late afternoon and Tate sat up, looking around, rubbing the neck fur on Lobo, "Well boy, I really fell asleep, didn't I? Humm, wonder what them renegades have been up to." He stood and looked around, "Mebbe if we climb up on them rocks yonder, we can see down in the flats an' see what's goin' on, ya' reckon?" He retrieved his spyglass and started for the rocks. It was a rocky mound that appeared as a stack of moss covered boulders, with a tenacious piñion growing from a crack. As they scrambled to the topmost boulder, he saw a break in the tall pines that gave him a view of the flats. He sat down and drew up his knees to rest his elbows and Lobo lay on his belly at his side. He first searched the draw with the greenery where the renegades started into when he saw them by the fading light of the moon. With the aid of the scope, he searched every cut, every ravine, every arroyo that led into that draw, and there was nothing moving, no sign of renegades or white men.

He expanded his search to follow the draw back toward the tree line, looking for the renegade camp, the one he passed in the night. Scanning the tree tops for smoke and any opening in the trees for sign of movement, he saw nothing. He looked to the sky to determine how much light was left in the day and considered. He didn't know if the renegades had found Bear or if the man had escaped to continue his chase of the wagons. If he had, Tate knew he would have to pursue him to stop him. But if the renegades had taken Bear, he might be gathering the band for another attack. He looked to Lobo and said, "I think we'll need to check the draw down yonder to see if Bear and whoever is with him, are after the wagons or if the renegades took 'em. Don't you think that's best, too?" Lobo stood and wagged his tail, tongue lolling out, and pushed against Tate's leg.

THE MOON WAS WANING from full, but the clear night made his search of the draw easy. The remains of a camp were evident, with two saddles and one ragged blanket in a pile. With most Indians fashioning their own saddle or using nothing more than a blanket, saddles were seen as unnecessary. Tate knew the two men had been taken and were now captives of the renegades. He motioned for Lobo to follow the tracks of the renegades and the two started up from the draw toward the trees. He knew the camp of the Indians was farther to the east, but he thought they could take a trail through the black timber and approach unseen. He motioned to Lobo to come back alongside as they neared the tree line.

The first whiff of the stench of burning flesh brought Tate to a sudden halt. It's a smell that once recognized, seems to take root in the halls of remembrance and never leaves. Tate dropped to the ground, leaving Shady ground tied and taking Lobo as he carried his Hawken held across his chest, he started through the trees. He lifted his neckerchief to cover his mouth and nose as the stench grew stronger, and he slowly moved closer. A snap of a twig made him freeze, Lobo stopped and watched before them, still no movement, no sound. Moving from tree to tree, Tate worked through the timber coming closer to the site of the small village. There was no smell of smoke, no sign of movement, apparently the renegades had moved on. As he neared the edge of the clearing, the stench of burnt flesh was almost overwhelming. Then a low growl came, making Lobo drop into his attack stance, head low and teeth bared, as he carefully stepped forward. Suddenly the snapping of teeth and the growls and snarls of the two wolves encountered before came from near a stand of trees apart from the clearing.

Tate dropped a hand to keep Lobo from attacking and the two moved together as they neared the scene with the two wolves. The black wolf had sunk his teeth into the figure bound to the trees and was tearing away the burnt flesh. Tate recognized the blackened figures as the remains of Bear and Sully. As the wolves turned to their new threat, he leveled the Hawken readying his shot. But Lobo was not to be denied and leaped forward at the big black wolf and the two collided as each sought to get a grip on the other's throat. Snarling, growling and yipping came from both as they grappled and rolled together. When the grey wolf started to join in, Tate moved the muzzle just a mite and pulled the trigger. The explosion split the night and the darkness made even darker by the smoke that belched from the big Hawken. The noise startled the black wolf and he quickly slunk away and ran into the trees. Lobo started to follow but a simple, "No!" from Tate stopped the beast.

As he stared at the gruesome sight, Tate was reminded *Vengeance is mine; I will repay, saith the Lord.* It was an arduous task, but Tate felt compelled to bury the bodies of the two men. When he finished, he looked at the two mounds, and said, "Lord, I know it probably seems a little odd, but I thank you. I think this is the last of it and now the folks on the wagon train can quit looking over their shoulders all the time. So, thank You." He dropped his head and with a snap of his fingers summoned Lobo. They returned to the camp in the trees, loaded the pack-horse and started after the wagons by the light of the moon.

CHAPTER THIRTY
RETURN

As Tate neared the Sweetwater, he began searching for a low bank, a sandbar, and deep backwater. With the twisting course of the river, he soon found what he was looking for and reined up and tethered the horses. He took a bar of lye soap from the parfleche and jumped into the deep, still pool of the backwater. He hollered to Lobo, "Come'on boy, you stink just as much as me! Them burnt bodies didn't do neither one of us any good. Come'on!" As Tate slapped the water, the big wolf leaped from the grassy bank and belly flopped next to the man, splashing him with a frothy wave. Tate was liberal in his use of the soap, lathering his buckskins before ducking under and taking them off to toss them on the bank. He did the same with his union suit and then started on Lobo. The big wolf wasn't too happy with the suds but endured them just to play in the water with Tate. The horses had been a little skittish with the smell of death about them, and even more so with the stench of burnt flesh, but they had given in, although somewhat begrudgingly. Tate was certain both horses would be a lot happier with both him and Lobo smelling a little fresher. After climbing from the water, Tate decided to spend the remaining hours of night and early morning camped by the willows of the river.

The reflected sunlight from the bathing pool brought him awake with the realization the sun was well up in the sky and they needed to get on the trail. The early morning breezes had accommodated him by drying out the union suit and making his buckskins tolerable. He took time for some coffee, having done without for the last couple of days, and he even fried up some of the smoked meat. Both Lobo and Tate were showing happy grins as they finally started on the trail after the wagons.

He passed the split rock and the stone-faced mound just before midday. By the time his hunger made him stop for the late meal, the sun was directly in front and blazing hot on his face. He found a thick cluster of alder and chokecherry, tethered the horses and withdrew his bow and slipped the quiver over his shoulder to hunt for some fresh meat. He soon returned, dragging a carcass of a small mule deer buck, and busied himself with preparing his meal with some fresh meat. Lobo was happy to help by disposing of the scraps and Tate tossed a couple of turnips in the coals to complete his meal. With fresh coffee, thinly seared venison steak, and baked turnips, Tate took special pleasure in his wilderness cooking.

When the sun dipped below the western horizon, Tate and company were back on the trail. He knew he wasn't too far behind the wagons and thought he might catch up before dark or at least by first light of morning. And it was just before first light when Tate rode up to the wagons, he was challenged by someone on guard with, "Stop where you are!" He reined up and raised his hands as the figure approached from the dark shadows of the wagons. Tate could see the man held a rifle before him and he waited. When he was closer, the voice called, "Is that you Tate?" Tate recognized the voice as that of Mark, the young man that he had instructed in the ways of a scout.

"Yeah, is that you Mark?" answered Tate as he slowly lowered his hands.

"Boy, if you ain't a sight for sore eyes. We'd almost given up on you. C'mon, I'm sure Ma's gonna be glad enough to see you that she'll wanna feedju too."

Although Tate had stopped for a short rest in the darkest part of the night, he hadn't eaten since his meal of venison and the thought of a meal cooked by Ruth Hillyard was appealing. She was known for her dutch oven biscuits and Tate hankered for one or two. He stepped down from his saddle, tethered his horses to the nearby wagon, loosened the cinches, and followed Mark to the middle of the wagons, just beginning to stir with activity.

"Hey ever'body! Look who I found wanderin' around in the dark!" hollered Mark as he gestured toward Tate. Several came to welcome Tate back and others just hollered their greetings and waved their welcome. Mark had been right about his mom wanting to feed the welcome wanderer and she insisted he take a seat while she finished the meal preparations.

With the coming of first light, Tate looked around at the nearby terrain seeing an upthrust of rock that appeared as a massive grave of solid rock, and the river passing behind it. They had chosen their camp well, high ground, good visibility, and the rock behind them. He was proud of the farmers and how they had become accustomed to the ways of the trail. While the men waited for the cooking, Henry Hyde and Lucas walked over to greet Tate and talk a bit. "It sure is good to see you, Tate. We were gettin' a little concerned. Even got to wonderin' if you met up with Bear and company and had trouble," commented Henry.

Tate raised his hand a little and said, "You don't have to

worry about Bear and company anymore, or the renegades for that matter. That's all over with, and now we can keep our eyes toward the mountains."

The men looked at Tate, waiting for an explanation, but with none coming, Henry said, "Well, we've got a different concern. We've been followed by some Indians. Don't know how many or what tribe. Mark there saw the first sign, figgered there were anywhere from twelve to twenty, but all we've seen since is two or three, up on the skyline."

"Skyline? Well, that's a good thing. When they're lettin' themselves be seen, they're just lettin' you know they're watchin', kinda keepin' track of you and what you're doin'," explained Tate.

"You don't think they mean any harm then?" asked Lucas.

"Not unless you do."

"What'chu mean?" asked Lucas, his wrinkled forehead showing his confusion.

"Most Indians, 'cept them renegades of course, have a lot of respect for the land and all it holds. If you show that same respect, that sits well with 'em and they will normally not come callin'," answered Tate.

"I still don't understan'," replied Lucas.

"Well, take for example some o' those buffler hunters. There's gittin' to be more n' more of 'em since the market on beaver pelts has dropped, an' them fellas come out with big guns and wagons, kill a bunch of buffalo and take just the hides and leave carcasses to rot. Those are buffalo the Indians depend on for every aspect of their lives. Indians'll use just 'bout everything on a buffalo and when a white man just wastes it, that ain't respectful, and the Indians'll usually teach 'em a little respect by takin' a few scalps. But it's not just the buffalo, it's everything out here," he said, with a nod and a sweeping arm movement.

Their dialogue was interrupted by Ruth when she called,

"Breakfast is ready! Come an' get it!" Wes, Mark, and Tate stood and started to the fire as Henry and Lucas went to their wagons. Just a short while later the wagons were stretched out with the rising sun at their backs. Tate had explained they would soon be leaving the Sweetwater for a turn that would take them through the red hills toward South Pass, but there was a surprise waiting for them towards the end of the day's journey.

Although many tried to get Tate to divulge his surprise, he remained smug and mum as they traveled across the sage covered flats. It was late afternoon and with nothing remarkable in sight and no rock outcroppings for cover nor high ground to take, Tate motioned for the wagons to circle up and make camp for the night. The drivers of the wagons followed his lead but as they drew closer in the circle, they looked to one another with a touch of confusion and questioning expressions.

When everyone had unharnessed the animals and hobbled them on the grassy flat, Tate told the men, "Grab a spade and follow me, but watch your step," he looked at the women who were also anxious about the surprise and motioned for them to follow as well. Within about fifty yards of the wagons, they came to what appeared as a slough with floating clumps of moss and grass. The standing water appeared to be alkaline with the edges of the pools outlined in white residue. "Space out a little, don't everybody step on the same clump," cautioned Tate. When he came to an area with less standing water, he hopped up and down and the people were startled to see the ground shake around them. Tate laughed and motioned to Lucas, "Dig down here, oh, about a foot or so, maybe more, and see what you find," he lifted his eyes to the others as Lucas started digging at the thick peat moss, "the rest of you just wait till you see what he finds."

Beneath the thick moss, standing water surprised Lucas, but he bent down and thrust his spade and was surprised when it hit something hard. He used the spade to move the water aside and was even more surprised at what he saw. He looked up at Tate, grinned and started chopping with the spade and within moments, brought up a big chunk of clear ice. The others stood aghast at what he held, and he said, "It's ice! Clear as can be! Lot's of it!" The others began to chatter, and some began to dig as Lucas stood up and looked to Tate, "If the water's alkaline, how can this be any good?"

"Different water. That surface water shows alkaline because of the soil, but that ice is from an underground source. Indians have been usin' it for years!"

The men remembered what Tate had said earlier about respecting the land and Henry asked, "Well, do you think it'll be alright if we each take some?"

"Sure, it won't last too much longer anyway. I wasn't sure there'd even be any this late. Most o' the time, it's gone by mid-summer. That black moss keeps it frozen this long." After returning to the wagons, the people chattered about the discovery and enjoyed the ice added to their drinks as they talked about how great it would be to have lemons for cold lemonade and other concoctions that would be made all the better by some ice. It was a pleasant interlude to their travels and they gathered around when the preacher, Edmond Bowman, broke out

his fiddle and led the folks in a round of singing. The last song was "There's Nothing True but Heaven."

The world is all a fleeting show, for man's illusion giv'n;

The world is all a fleeting show, for man's illusion giv'n;

The smiles of joy, the tears of woe, Deceitful shine, deceitful flow,

There's nothing true, but Heav'n,

There's nothing true, but Heav'n,

There's nothing true, but Heav'n!
And false the light on glory's plume, as fading hues of even;
And false the light on glory's plume, as fading hues of even;
And love, and hope, and beauty's bloom, are blossoms gather'd
for the tomb.
There's nothing bright but heav'n,
There's nothing bright but heav'n,
There's nothing bright but heav'n!

Everyone turned in for the evening, with thoughts of heaven running through their minds, but Tate wasn't in a hurry to get there so he made certain Mark and Jason would take first and second watch and he would finish the night out. Although they hadn't seen any Indians on this day's journey, it would still be best to be cautious.

CHAPTER THIRTY-ONE
STORM

AFTER THE BATTLE WITH THE RENEGADES AND THE LOSS OF THE
Heaton and Webster couples, the people condensed the items
from their two wagons into one. They took spare parts from
the wagon left behind and used the extra wagon for excess
baggage, including the gear and supplies of Tate that were
usually carried by his second packhorse. That also gave the
group four additional mules to switch off with any of their
mules that came up lame or needed to be given a time of rest.
Tate had encouraged the farmer families to be extra vigilant
with the condition of their animals as the pulling would get
more difficult when they entered the foothills of the Wind
River mountain range. Extra attention was paid to the condition of the the hooves, legs and general state.

After leaving the ice slough, they also left the Sweetwater
valley. Tate had taken over the scout, leaving Mark and
Cassie to handle the spare wagon and Jason to take the backtrail scout. With the terrain reasonably flat, Tate had taken
sight on a distant mountain that rose just above a series of
colorful clay ridges. His chosen route would take them north
of that point after they dropped into a red rock canyon. He

knew it would be approaching dark when they reached that canyon, if they made good time throughout the day.

Lobo was trotting beside Shady when they dropped into a swale with a narrow creek in the bottom. Rabbit brush and sage dotted the slope above the creek, but in the bottom and near the water was grass and a few stunted chokecherry bushes. Tate reined up and slipped to the ground, letting Shady take a drink of the cool water.

"Ya' know Lobo, I ain't liking them clouds." He looked to see if the wolf was paying any attention and continued, "Look at those big uns boilin' over there. Especially that big black one that sittin' right over where we're goin', nossir, I don't like that'n at all. 'Tween here n' there, ain't much cover an' if that's a bad storm . . . " he let the thought drop as he continued watching the churning clouds. He looked to Shady grazing by the stream as he sat on a large sandstone boulder, thinking. The rattle of trace chains brought his head around to see the approach of the wagons with the lead wagon driven by Gertrude Pickett, who had repeatedly proven herself the equal of any of the men.

Tate stood and directed the farmers to line out and pull up for their noon break and watched as the eight wagons pulled to a stop and the drivers stepped down. Each man helped his wife to find her footing from the wagon box to the wheel hub and down, but Gertrude didn't wait for Jeffrey. The women busied themselves digging into their stores at the rear of the wagons while the men unhooked the mules, one at a time, from the single trees and led them to water. Tate noticed several of the men looking at the clouds and probably thinking the same thing as he had been dwelling upon.

Henry Hyde, ever the leader, walked to Tate's side and motioned toward the billowing clouds and said, "You think that's gonna hit us?"

"Well, it's sittin' right over where we're goin', so, probably," answered Tate.

"Didju see those Indians?" asked Henry.

"Yeah, I saw a couple of 'em sittin' their horses, quite a ways north of the trail. They were too far away to get a good look and by the time I got to my spyglass, they were gone.But, honestly, I'm more concerned about that storm. The only cover to speak of is a canyon right under those clouds, nothin' between here and there."

"Well, I don't think it'll hurt us to get a little wet. After all these hot sunny days, it might be a nice change," suggested Henry.

"Maybe if we make this a short stop and make good time after we pull out, we might get to some cover. But you're right, a little water never hurt anybody. Course, in this country, ya' always gotta be watchful for flash floods," answered Tate, pondering the possibilities. The thought of flash floods made him look upstream of the swale where they were watering the animals, and to the small ravines that fed this little creek. He recognized this as a perfect place for a disaster if a flash flood came, but with no rain nearby, he believed them to be safe for now.

In less than an hour, the wagons were back on the move. Everyone was aware of the coming storm and the slight possibility of finding shelter, and all were anxious to find cover. Tate was again on the scout well ahead of the wagons and the dim trail occasionally had to be marked. This was done with a stack of rocks and a marker of an arrow in stones, showing the course.

"UP AND DOWN, up and down, one gulley after 'nother'n. With all this flat land, a person'd think he could find a trail that was easier on our mules!" complained Gertrude, never known for her complimentary remarks.

"I'm sure he's takin' the best way, darlin'," answered the meek-mannered Jeffrey.

"Hummph. Sometimes I wonder if that kid even knows which end is up!" she grumbled as she slapped the reins to her mules' rumps and hollered at them to climb from the arroyo. Having surrendered the lead to Felix and Angelique Robidoux, Gertrude thought it necessary to hang back from the lead wagon to keep from their dust. As the mules topped out from the arroyo, she choked away some dust and lifted her scarf around her mouth and nose, mumbling, "A little water from them clouds might at least cut down on this dust!"

THE WISPY CURTAIN of water was trailing behind the towering clouds like a bridal train and the wagons and water were on a direct course toward one another. The wind had cooled and increased as Tate crammed his hat down and ducked his head to shield his face from the increasing bluster. Shady's mane whipped at his face and he gave the horse his head as they trudged toward the creek bottom of Beaver Creek. If they could make it, and it wasn't flooding, they could follow the creek upstream to the deeper canyon that could give some shelter.

Then the rain hit. Gentle at first and even welcome, as the wind seemed to slow, and it brought a comfortable cool. Even the animals seemed to welcome the refreshing change as they lifted their heads and wagged their ears. Tate hollered to the Robidouxs, "Pick up the pace, we're almost there!" But the increasing rain renewed the force of the wind and his words were carried away with the storm. The intensity of the storm increased, and the rain appeared to fall in sheets, pooling on the clay soil and making footing for the mules difficult. The mules leaned into their traces, ducking their heads before the rain, and dug in their hooves as bidden by the drivers.

Suddenly, the rain was mixed with hail and white ice balls began pelting the bonnets of the wagons and the backs of the mules. Most of the women left the seats beside their husbands and ducked back under the canvas covers. Shady started kicking as if he could strike back at the offending hail, but to no avail. Tate saw the size of the hailstones was increasing and within moments, balls the size of turnips pelted the mules and they protested.

Suddenly pandemonium overtook the wagon train. Mules were braying, kicking, trying to buck and free themselves of the restraining harness and the drag of the wagons. The team of the lead wagon, held by Felix Robidoux, broke from his control and started running with each of the four mules protesting, kicking, and braying as their long ears took blow after blow. Felix propped his feet against the front of the wagon box and leaned back against the reins, pulling for all his worth, but the mules just bowed their necks and ran.

Tate saw the dilemma and slapped leather to Shady as he chased the runaway wagon. Within moments, he drew alongside the lead mules, leaned over and grabbed the reins. As he pulled back on the reins of Shady, he leaned back, pushing against the extended stirrups and sought to pull up on the stubborn and frightened mules. Shady stumbled against the mule, caught his footing and with Tate letting up on the reins, the horse kept pace with the mules. Tate again pulled on the leads of the team and the mules started to slow. He spoke to them, having to almost holler, but he tried to soothe the terrified animals. Suddenly the mule pulled towards Shady and the two tangled their feet causing Shady to stumble and unseat Tate.

The man flew from his seat, over the head of his horse, but was brought to a sudden stop when his foot, caught in the stirrup stayed his flight. Both horse and rider fell into the mud, and kicked at one another, trying to right themselves. Shady was the first to stand, and with legs spread and his body shaking, he watched as Tate struggled to his feet, shaking the mud from his arms and wiping it from his face. Tate looked at his horse, saw the wagon stopped on the other side of him, and then he looked Shady over to ensure his faithful mount was unhurt. He was pleased to see the grulla's only injuries were the same as his, both had injured pride. He laughed as he reached for the muddy reins, patted Shady on his neck and said, "Let's go check on the other wagons, shall we boy? By the way, where's Lobo?" But he didn't have to look far as a drenched wolf stood no more than ten paces away, looking as if he was laughing at the muddy pair. It was only then that Tate noticed the hail had surrendered to a steady downpour of rain. He mounted up and started back along the line of wagons. Although all had a bit of a tussle with their mules, none were damaged, and everyone was anxious to continue to the promised cover. By dusk, the rain had ceased, and the clouds moved away to give the promise of a better day to come. The wagons found their shelter in the lee of a tall bluff of red clay and sandstone with grass aplenty between the bluff and Beaver Creek. The appearance of a mud-caked Tate and an equally muddy Shady gave the farmers the silver lining of laughter to the black cloud of the storm.

THE NEXT DAY, AFTER A WAIT OF A COUPLE HOURS FOR THE
warm sun and wind to do the work of drying out the clay
soil, the wagons were on their way. It was a long slow pull up
a gradual slope before they crossed over a ridge and down to
cross the upper waters of Beaver Creek. With more of the
same up and down travel across the ravine scarred flats, they
reached the arrow point of land that separated the headwaters of Beaver Creek and the deeper red canyon that showed
more color than the setting sun. As the wagons circled to
make camp atop the wide plateau, Tate pointed out the Wind
River mountains and the cut that held the South Pass. Tate
thought he detected a group sigh of relief from the people
when they realized this had long been a distant goal for
them. And to know they were within sight of the last major
landmark of their journey, meant they were nearing their
ultimate destination and the end of their long journey.

"I didn't see any Indians today, did'ju?" asked Henry Hyde
as he strolled towards Tate. The others had left the group to
begin their preparations for the evening meal and other
duties. Tate was making his usual camp apart from the

wagons and was rolling out his bedroll next to a circle of stones he had prepared for his cookfire.

"No, I didn't," answered Tate, continuing with his camp preparations.

"What do you suppose that means?" inquired Henry.

"Hard to say. I'm not sure if they were Cheyenne or Arapaho or . . . " he answered, "but with nothing else to consider, I'd say they gave up watching and went back to wherever their village was, probably no longer concerned about us." He stood and motioned with a wide sweep of his arm, "Where we are is mostly Arapaho territory. However, Cheyenne, Crow, even some Sioux are known to raid and hunt in this country. South of here, you get into Ute country, but I don't think we need to worry 'bout them. Now, as we go over South Pass, that's Arapaho territory."

"Are they hostile?" asked Henry.

"Any Indians can be hostile." Tate looked at Henry, sat down on a rock, and began, "See, Indians aren't like us, although they have chiefs and such, it's not an absolute rule, like with an army or whatever. Among the native people, anytime a young buck or sub-chief gets a hankerin', he can gather others and go on a hunt or a raid. All it takes is one warrior with an idea and others that want to follow, and you've got a raiding party, or a hunting party that could turn into a raiding party.

Now, if that leader's little get together is unsuccessful, then next time most of the others won't follow him. But, if they have a good hunt or a raid that brings lots of plunder and captives, then next time he gets one together, then more will follow. They put great value on honors gained by a successful hunt and raid. Each warrior that draws blood, gets honors, and even counting coup gains honors. The more honors, the higher they rise on the ladder of becoming a chief."

"Interesting. Now, what if the chief or leaders or what-ever, tell the young bucks not to go, then what?" asked an interested Henry.

"Well, seldom does a chief actually forbid such action. But if he does, then the young buck best mind, cuz if he don't, then the chief and elders can discipline him. Like, kick him out of the village, like those renegades that we fought."

"Well, thanks for the education, Tate. See ya' in the mornin'," declared Henry as he turned back to rejoin the wagons.

It was a pleasant night and Tate lay with hands behind his head as he stared at the stars and listened to the love-sick coyotes serenading one another. When he first joined up with the wagon train, he had promised them he would be with them only as far as South Pass, anything further would be entirely up to them. When he told Henry Hyde about the wide and fertile valley of the Green River beyond the pass, Henry had quizzed him for every detail and had expressed an interest in settling in the area. Not that Tate was anxious to see a permanent settlement in the area, he preferred that all the settlers move farther west and leave his country to the Indians and the buffalo, but as he thought about having these farmers as neighbors, he thought it wouldn't be all bad. After all, the valley of the Green was at least a week's travel away. He rolled over, stroked the fur on Lobo's neck and said, "Let's get us some sleep, shall we?" Lobo's only answer was a raised eyebrow.

It would be a long day of hard pulling and Tate rousted everyone out before first light. Many thought there was an attack or something that caused the man to shake the wagons to bring them awake, but when they stuck sleepy eyed heads out, they were told, "Long day ahead, we need to get started. Don't take time for breakfast, we'll take a break soon 'nuff. Let's hook 'em up and head 'em up, long way to go and need to be movin'!"

Although they grumbled all the while, the men soon had the mules harnessed and hooked up, ready to start the long pull up South Pass. None of the people had experienced mountains and even the biggest hills of Missouri were nothing more than bumps in the road compared to the Rocky Mountains. Their first view of the granite crags and rocky slopes of the towering mountains, even these in the lower end of the Wind River range, held the travelers spellbound. To see the patches of white still holding to the mountains in the heat of the summer was incomprehensible to the flatlanders. When they drew in lungs full of sweet pine scented mountain air, they revelled in the moment.

Jason and Charly had taken the wagon previously driven by Mark and Cassie and now, mounted and riding with Tate, Mark said, "I'm beginning to see what you love about these mountains. They're beautiful!"

Cassie added, "And the air's so, so, clean and fresh! I love the smell of those pines!"

Tate grinned at the two greenhorns and answered, "Yeah, it's something that gets into your spirit. Either ya' love it or ya' hate it. Some folks can't hardly breath when they get higher in the mountains and some flatlanders feel crowded by the thick pines. But others feel that way about all the thick woods back east and all the people make it crowded. My Pa and I read everything we could about the mountains, even the ledgers of Lewis and Clark. Everything we learned, whether something we read or heard about from those that had been here, just made us want to see it more. When my Pa died, I just took off and came to see for myself. Best thing I ever did!"

"But haven't you ever wanted a home? You know, someplace to live and raise a family?" asked Cassie, hopeful of an answer even to her unspoken questions.

Tate waved his arm toward the black timber and the distant mountains, "This is my home. As to the rest of your question, my wife and I have a home back up there in those mountains, yonder," nodding with his head. "She's waiting for me."

"Oh, I didn't know. I just assumed you weren't married. But you have a home there?" she asked.

"We built a cabin up there. It sits back in the trees, we used to sit on the front porch and look down at the lake below. Quite often we'd see a herd of elk come down and water at the north end of the lake, she loved that." His eyes had glazed over as he remembered and pictured the image of his mate. He dropped his head and looked back at the trail, and up the hill beyond.

Cassie had noted the past tense of his descriptions and wondered, "Her name?" she asked.

Tate smiled at the memory and said, "White Fawn."

"Oh, she was Indian?" said Cassie, asking the obvious question. She wanted to know more, to know everything about her, but she was hesitant to pry more.

"Ummmhummm," answered Tate, without explanation. He gigged his horse forward to pull away from the questioning woman, not wanting to share his private thoughts and grief. He felt tears coming, dabbed at his eyes with his sleeve, and spoke to Lobo, "Scout boy, go!" The wolf gave a quick glance to Tate and started off at a run to explore the trail before them. Tate knew if there was anything to be concerned about, Lobo would find it and return to warn him. Right now, he just wanted a little time alone and turned from the trail to explore the trees on the upside of the hill north of the trail.

He moved wide of the wagon's trail, cutting through the

pines and into a large thicket of aspen. He found a narrow game trail that paralleled the lower road and followed the path. He stepped down from his saddle and walked before his horse, examining the sign on the trail. Usually, there would only be tracks of wildlife, deer, elk, bear, wolves and others, but there were clear tracks of recent passing of horses. Tate knew there were a few small herds of wild mustangs in this country, but these tracks were made by hooves that had been trimmed but not shod. Indians. As he examined the tracks, it was impossible to tell how many had passed, but there were several. Hopefully, just a small hunting party.

Tate swung back aboard and pointed Shady downhill to catch the wagon trail again. The grulla dropped his rear and stiffened his front legs as they slid down the steep slope to the trail. He lifted Shady's head as they gained solid footing and started to turn up the road when Lobo came trotting back. His mouth was not open, and his stance told of trouble. Tate leaned on Shady's neck with his elbow, looked down at Lobo as Shady turned his head toward his friend, and asked, "What is it boy? What'dja see?" Lobo answered with a low growl, turned back to lead the way up the trail, looking over his shoulder to his master. Tate called to him, "Wait a minute, boy. Here come the wagons, I need to talk to them first."

HENRY HYDE WAS IN THE LEAD WAGON AND WAS GREETED BY Tate with a hand up, palm forward, to have him stop. Tate said, "There might be trouble up ahead. I saw Indian sign in the trees and Lobo's showing trouble, so, take it easy, but keep coming. You might pass word back for everybody to have their rifles handy, just in case. But don't go shootin' 'till I say, alright?"

"Are there very many?" asked Henry, obviously distraught at the thought of another Indian fight.

"Don't know yet, don't even know if they're around close, but, I'm gonna be checkin' it out, so just be prepared." Without giving Hyde a chance for any more questions, Tate wheeled about and started after Lobo at a trot. They were nearing the crest of the pass and the trees were farther back from the trail, leaving the area well exposed and with little cover. Tate pulled Shady to a walk as he slowly gained sight of the flat at the top of the pass. As he crested the flat top and searched the level plain, about a quarter mile between the trees, showed nothing.

Tate visibly relaxed but watched Lobo as he began to carefully pick his steps, eyes on the tree line to the right. With a low growl, Lobo dropped his head and walking toward the trees, he moved back and forth searching. Tate knew the wolf had spotted danger, but he couldn't see the cause. Then a flash of color showed between the trees and mounted Indians came at a walk from the timber. They emerged, one or two at a time, and took up position making a barrier line across the flat and across the wagon trail. Tate had reined to a stop and watched, knowing he had been seen. He guessed there were about twenty, all warriors, some with lances, shields and bows, and a few with rifles proudly displayed by standing them with the rifle butts on their thighs and muzzles in the air. Tate noted the absence of war paint and with knee pressure, moved his mount forward, keeping Lobo in check and alongside. When he was within about sixty yards, he stopped, looking from warrior to warrior. He was certain these were Arapaho.

WHEN HENRY HYDE'S wagon crested the pass, he saw movement ahead and slowed the wagon without stopping. As he neared, he was surprised to see Tate riding slowly towards a line of Indians. Henry pulled his wagon to a stop, but the other wagons pulled alongside as space allowed. Lucas asked Henry in a low voice, "What's he doin'?"

"I dunno, but there ain't been no shootin' so far." He reached down and grabbed his rifle, laying it across his lap. He glanced and saw the frizen up and realized he needed to put powder in the pan to ready his rifle and reached for his powder horn.

Edmond Bowman's wagon pulled even with Henry's as Edmond asked, "What's happening?" Henry just nodded toward the flat and continued readying his rifle. Edmond was startled by the line of Indians, looked to Henry and then to his own rifle. He lifted it to check the load and primer, satisfied, he sat it back in the corner of the wagon box and looked to their scout.

As Tate looked at the many warriors, he saw some that seemed a little familiar, but as his eyes came to the middle of the line, he recognized the apparent leader of the band. A slow grin crossed his face as he looked at the stoic warriors trying to intimidate their opponent with stern expressions. But Tate knew their tactic and started Shady forward and with a snap of his fingers, Lobo moved beside his friend. Tate chuckled to himself, anxious to see his friend and urged Shady to a trot. As he neared the line, several of the warriors' mounts shied back from Lobo, but their riders controlled them as they too looked at the big wolf that trotted by this white man. When Tate was within twenty feet, he raised his hand, palm forward and greeted the Indian in their native tongue, "Little Raven! My brother, it does my heart good to see you."

Little Raven had recognized Tate as much by the horse he rode as by his appearance. This was the man he had traveled to see and was glad to greet the man who had taken his sister as a mate. Raven and his band had been on a hunt, but his main purpose was to see his sister again. They had been to the cabin and Raven saw the grave and knew his sister had crossed over, but he wanted to see Tate before they returned to their village. The entire village had traveled south, and the families and lodges had been encamped near the red canyon. Beyond the canyon was a migratory route for buffalo and this was the mid-summer hunt for the wooly beasts. Their roundabout route was to try to come into the valley behind the herd and improve their chances for a good hunt. Raven had chosen to seek out his sister and her man to have them join the hunt.

"Greetings my brother," answered Raven. His horse had sidestepped at the appearance of Lobo, but Tate's hand signal dropped the wolf to his belly and the horses settled down.

"What brings my wife's people to our home?" asked Tate.

"It is our buffalo hunt. We go to the way they travel. We came to have you join us, but we saw the marker at your lodge," answered Raven.

Tate's head dropped, and he began to explain, "She took sick in the winter. The coughing disease, she fought long but it took her. It was the coming of the green time."

Raven's head lifted as he understood. "My heart is heavy for you." He looked past Tate to see the wagons and said, "I see you travel with others." Tate twisted in his saddle to see the wagons, turned back and answered, "They are traveling through. They plan to go far," motioning to the west, "and make their homes beyond the land of the Arapaho. Maybe closer to the Paiute."

Raven looked at his brother and shook his head, "They will not live long among the Paiute."

"Yes, the Paiute are a hard people, but these are hard too. They fought renegades and killed many and still they come. But I will go no further. I am home." He motioned to the trees in the direction of his cabin and added, "This is where I will be." Tate turned back toward the wagons, and looked to Raven, "Join us. We will fix a meal and talk."

Raven nodded, motioned to his men, and the entire band fell in line behind the two friends as they started toward the wagons.

WHEN HENRY and the others saw Tate leading the Indians toward them he said, "Now what's he doin'?"

"Well, if it's like he did with them Cheyenne, looks like he done invited 'em to supper," answered Lucas, chuckling. "If that don't beat all, here we're thinkin' we're in for another fight, and he invites 'em to supper."

Lucas' suspicions were confirmed when Tate reined up in front of the wagons and said, "Folks, I want you to meet my brother-in-law! This here's Little Raven, the leader of the Arapaho. I've invited these fellas to supper, so, if'n you don't mind, how 'bout circlin' up and start cookin'? We'll probably spend a day or two here, so we'll be able to fill your larders with fresh meat, so don't worry 'bout usin' up what'chu got left."

While the wagons circled up and began their preparations, the Indians took to the tree line to picket their horses. When they returned, the warriors made a fire and gathered around, using their blankets for ground cover as they awaited the meal. The women of the wagons, recalling their experience with the Cheyenne, knew the warriors would expect to be served but their men pitched in to help and the meal was soon ready.

Although Gertrude complained, she was stilled by Sylvia Bowman, the preacher's wife, when she said, "Personally, I prefer cooking to digging graves. How 'bout you Gertrude?" She received a scowl in answer, but at least the woman quit complaining. Some of the warriors walked among the wagons, looking at the gear and people of the wagon train, but with little understanding of the other's language, communication was difficult. Sylvia saw one of the warriors watching as she opened her dutch oven of biscuits and his smile prompted Sylvia to put a little honey on one and offer it to the man. When he took his first bite, he grinned widely, said something in Arapaho, and walked away happy. Sylvia grinned at the compliment, even though she didn't understand the words.

TRUE TO HIS WORD, Tate had the wagons stay camped for another day while he took the young people on a hunt to replenish their meat supply. Jason, Mark and the girls, Charly and Cassie were happy when he invited them, and they were eager for the adventure. Jason had told Tate of Mark's thoughts about staying in the mountains and Tate wanted to give him a taste of mountain living.

Tate had loaded all of his gear and supplies on his two pack-horses, planning on leaving everything at his cabin, and started off in the lead of the small group heading into the trees. It was a couple of hours later when they came within sight of the lake. An opening in the pines revealed the blue water below and Tate reined up to point out the picturesque sight.

"Is that the lake where you and your wife watched the elk?" asked Cassie.

"Yes, it is. Our cabin is back in the trees yonder," nodding his head to the west of the lake. "We'll be there in a few minutes."

At the edge of the lake, the trail turned toward the cabin although it wasn't visible from this part of the lake. When they broke into the clearing, everyone reined up and looked at the scene of the well-constructed cabin, the corrals and sheds for the horses, and the sloping clearing below the porch.

Cassie stood in her stirrups and looked back in the direction of the lake and could easily visualize the two sitting on the porch and enjoying the view. She looked at Tate, saw the emotion on his face and motioned to the others to follow. She moved her horse along the tree line toward the corral and stepped down to tie the horse to the pole fence. The others followed, no one speaking, giving Tate a few solitary moments.

Tate soon joined them at the fence, turned his horses into the corral and began derigging the packs and saddles. He said, "Go on, look around. Cabin's not locked. I'll be along in a minute. Oh, hey, Mark, grab one o' those packs and take it inside, will ya'?"

"Glad to," replied Mark as he walked to the packs. He motioned for Jason to grab one too and each of the young men carried a pack and a parfleche around the corner to the porch of the cabin. When Tate joined them, he carried the remaining packs and parfleche, dropped them on the porch and turned to look at the lake below. His shoulders lifted in a deep sigh as he gazed at the still water, remembering.

The young people felt a little uncomfortable, not knowing what to say, but Tate soon stirred them to action. "Fellas, how 'bout you goin' into the trees yonder and fetching a little firewood. Ladies, if you'll look in that pack there," motioning to a pack near the door, "you'll find some fixin's and what-have-you and you can use the fireplace in yonder and maybe fix a little bit to eat 'fore we go explorin', if that's alright." The girls smiled and nodded as they waved at the boys heading to the trees for the firewood. While the youngsters were busy with their assigned tasks, Tate visited the grave of White Fawn, savoring a few moments with his memories.

After their simple meal of thin sliced pork belly fried with some cornpone, Tate suggested the couples pair off and take a walk around the lake. "Be sure to take your rifle with you, ya' never know when you might meet up with a neighborhood grizz.'"

The girls looked to see if Tate was kidding them and saw a serious expression that spoke caution and Cassie asked, "Grizz?"

"Yup. There are a few Grizzly bears in this country." At the questioning looks, he asked, "You ain't never seen a Grizzly bear, have you?"

Four heads shook in the negative as if they were tied to a string like four puppets. Tate began to explain, "Well, good thing about a grizz, you won't mistake 'em. They are the biggest things in the woods. But, if you see one, don't run, cuz' you can't outrun one."

"Uh, how big are they, and if we can't run what do we do?" asked Charly.

Tate looked around and looking at the beams overhead, motioned toward them and said, "See those beams there? Well if a big boar grizzly was to stand on his hind feet like they're known to do, he could swat the beam and break it in two without so much as a by your leave."

The young people gaped open-mouthed at the beam that was about eight feet from the floor and Cassie asked, "So, if we can't run, what do we do, climb a tree?"

"Oh no, bears can climb faster'n you, they got claws, remember? No, your best bet is to just lay down and pretend you're dead."

"Won't he still attack us?" asked Jason.

"Yeah, but if you stay still like you're dead, he'll lose interest and leave."

Tate could tell the young people were a little frightened and he could keep a straight face no longer and let a chuckle escape as he said, "Well, even though there have been grizz in these mountains, I don't think you'll have any trouble with one. They usually stay pretty shy of anything that has to do with people. But, if you're goin', take your rifle anyway. You might see a deer, or an elk and your folks are expecting you to bring back some meat."

Tate had cautioned them to stay away from the inlet as he was hoping to see some elk come down and by mid-afternoon both couples had returned to the cabin, enthusiastic from their walk in the woods. Cassie said, "We saw a doe and a fawn, several squirrels and rabbits, and an osprey nest atop a big ol' snag of a tree. It's so beautiful in the woods and around the lake. I've never been anyplace prettier." Mark grinned at her comments, nodding his head in agreement.

Charly chimed in with, "We saw a fox and her kits, and I think we saw a black bear too!"

Tate smiled at the two couples and said, "What else?"

Mark said, "That little stream coming off the slope yonder, there were a couple of beaver ponds. At least I think that's what they were."

Tate nodded in agreement as Jason added, "I didn't see any other animals, but I saw some big tracks. They were like deer tracks, only bigger and wider."

"Were they by the water or in the trees?" asked Tate.

"Down by the low water at the edge of the lake," answered Jason.

"Probably a moose. There's a few of 'em around here. They like to wade into the water and eat the growth along the bottom."

Tate looked at the sky, and pointed out to the couples, "Dusk is comin' soon, so let's work our way around toward the inlet and maybe we can get an elk or two for the wagons."

TATE WAS IN THE LEAD, TRAILING HIS HEAVY-LADEN PACK-horses. With the carcasses of two young bull elk to pack out, Tate had to divide the load between the pack-horses and lesser portions to each of the ridden horses. The elk would provide almost nine hundred pounds of meat that was much needed by the people of the wagons. He knew the elk meat would be a nice change in their normal fare and he was certain all the people would greatly enjoy it.

Dusk was settling over the mountains as they moved along the dim trail to the top of South Pass. It was well after dark when they rode up to the wagons and were greeted by the anxious parents of the young people. Cassie and Charly couldn't stop talking about their hunting trip with Tate and the boys, and Jason and Mark were quick to boast that they were the ones that killed the elk. Tate leaned against the wagon, silently watching and enjoying, as the others unloaded the meat. Sylvia Bowman came to him and said, "We saved supper for you, now come on and join us. Those girls won't shut up unless you come, so c'mon now." She waved her hand in a come-along motion and turned away, expecting him to follow. He nodded his head and followed the woman to the table by the fire ring.

It was an enjoyable meal with the family and, as expected, the talkative girls shared all the details of their adventure. When they started talking about grizzly bears, Tate chuckled and listened to their repetition of his stories. Edmond looked at Tate and asked, "Have you ever had a run-in with a grizzly?"

"You might say that. One of 'em tried to eat me, but I convinced him otherwise," said the young mountain man with a droll expression. He offered no other explanation, much to the disappointment of the girls. When they insisted, he pushed the tunic and union suit off his shoulder and pointed to several ugly scars as he said, "That was his first bite." The girls oohed and ahhed, but no further details were forthcoming.

Tate stood and thanked Mrs. Bowman for the meal and began his round of goodbyes. He went from wagon to wagon and family to family, speaking to each one, giving guidance when asked, but mainly just expressing his thanks for their friendship and the time together. As he headed to his horses, everyone had gathered together to see him off and when he turned to see the group, his grin of appreciation was replaced with a catch in his throat and his eyes began to water. He dropped his head, turned to mount up and stepped easily into the stirrup to swing his leg over Shady's rump. He looked at the crowd and said, "I know you folks are gonna do well wherever you stop and I want you to know, I will think of you often and pray for you every time the Lord brings you to mind."

Most of the women were daubing at their eyes as they waved goodbye to this very special friend. Many of the ladies had sort of taken Tate under their wing as a protective mother, something Tate responded well to, especially when they fed him fresh baked dutch oven biscuits. Now they felt they were waving goodbye to one of their own sons, and tears came readily. The men knew they had learned much from the young man and were proud to call him their friend as they waved into the darkness as the dim light from the fires faded.

Tate lifted his eyes to the big half-moon, scanned the heavens and the familiar stars, and sucked in a deep breath of sweet smelling pine. He listened to the night sounds and smiled. He planned on a day or two at the cabin, then he might join Little Raven on their buffalo hunt. He would be back at the cabin before midnight and there was plenty for him to do around his cabin and the homeplace, what with it being neglected for several months. But for now, he just wanted some time alone with White Fawn.

A LOOK AT TIMBERLINE TRAIL (ROCKY MOUNTAIN SAINT BOOK 5) BY B.N. RUNDELL

Tate Saint, man of the mountains, was grieving his wife when Jim Beckwourth brought word from Kit Carson that he was needed at Bent's Fort. Eager to put his loss behind him and anxious to know what his mentor and friend needed, Tate set out for the fort. He had been summoned to help a young woman, Maggie O'Shaunessy, find her father, a man that was searching for gold and riches in the high country of the Rockies. Begrudgingly accepting the job as combination caretaker, teacher and protector of a fiery redhead from the city, Tate and Maggie set out to comb the mountains for her last living relative.

Meeting the challenges of the wilderness with confrontations with grizzlies, mountains storms, renegade mountain men, and warring Indian tribes, Tate and Maggie rescue a young Indian maiden and set out to return her to her people. With a journey that takes them through the mountains and to the Bayou Salado, danger seems to always be at hand. Then they find sign of her father, and set out to follow his trail, a trail that leads through mountain valley, across the high country above timberline and down into the flats that are filled with Cheyenne, Crow and Yamparika Ute Indians. With conflict and danger their constant companion, the two young people are forced to turn to one another to survive and hopefully find the girl's father before it's too late.

AVAILABLE JULY 2018 FROM B.N. RUNDELL AND WOLFPACK PUBLISHING

ABOUT THE AUTHOR

Born and raised in Colorado into a family of ranchers and cowboys, B.N. Rundell is the youngest of seven sons. Juggling bull riding, skiing, and high school, graduation was a launching pad for a hitch in the Army Paratroopers. After the army, he finished his college education in Springfield, MO, and together with his wife and growing family, entered the ministry as a Baptist preacher.

Together, B.N. and Dawn raised four girls that are now married and have made them proud grandparents. With many years as a successful pastor and educator, he retired from the ministry and followed in the footsteps of his entrepreneurial father and started a successful insurance agency, which is now in the hands of his trusted nephew. He has also been a successful audiobook narrator and has recorded many books for several award-winning authors. Now finally realizing his life-long dream, B.N. has turned his efforts to writing a variety of books, from children's picture books and young adult adventure books, to the historical fiction and western genres.